First Stop Brooklyn
Dee-Dee Diamond

First Stop Brooklyn.
Alpha edition.
Copyright 2019 Dee-Dee Diamond.
Printed by Amazon.
Imprint: Sphirah
Cover image, "Cyclone," artist unknown.
DO NOT DUPLICATE.

ISBN: 9781080618910

**To contact the author, please email
deedeediamond808080@gmail.com.**

Sphirah is a progressive imprint. Many of our materials are freely distributed on the cloud at Sphirah.com, and our books are printed only to order. This reduces our impact on the environment, maximizes the proliferation of our artists, and keeps our works at a low cost. Our non-exclusive licensing agreements allow our artists to pursue distribution methods as they please. Sphirah was created by the writer, for the writer. Our only ambition is to spread the written word far and wide.

Warm Wishes,

Harrison Reed Gross
Founder & First Chair Poet

This is a book of fictionalized names, characters, incidents & businesses. They are the product of my imagination blended with my childhood experience in Brownsville, New York City. Any resemblance to actual persons, living or dead, is purely coincidental.

This book is dedicated with love to my publisher, Harrison Reed Gross, and all who inspired me to write.

—Dee-Dee Diamond

A selection of twenty-six short chronicles…

…on the life and times of Old Brooklyn.

The Butcher's Daughter

1968.

The crowd was overflowing the brand-new white pillared mansion. Rolls Royces, Mercedes, Jaguars and stretch limos filled the circular driveway and clogged the cul-de-sac's private road.

This party was held in a wealthy suburb, of the *nouveau-riche* Boomers that gave the Five Towns its reputation of excess in the last half of the 20th century. It was a showy, blaring, spare-no-expense happening. Invited were only the snobby couture-attired clique of spoiled young marrieds. My husband Howard was surely the only self-made entrepreneur in their crowd. We were building our own McMansion here. Believe me, this was our only passport to this exclusive party.

The festivities were in full bloom, as with a great air of pretended nonchalance, we danced into the crowded mass. We caught the disco beat and inhaled the plentiful grass fumes.

I was sipping on a glass of bubbly, between tokes, gyrating and waving acknowledgements to familiar faces in the room, when an unfamiliar blonde taps my shoulder.

"Aren't you Dee-Dee?"

"Yes," I answered, puzzled.

"I'm Hilda and we lived on the same block, on Chester Street, in Brownsville," she said, clasping my hands. Someone from Brownsville in this crowd... I couldn't believe it!

My old neighborhood was the poorest, shabbiest of all of Brooklyn. I looked her over—she was a tall, svelte Park Avenue type. I was silent as she kept mentioning my long-forgotten childhood friends, one by one. Still I couldn't place her. Then she leaned over to my ear and whispered, "I was short, fat and had a big Jewish nose then!" We both laughed at her confession, but truth be known I still could not remember her.

As it turned out, Hilda was a new divorcee and a cousin of the hostesses, David and Lola Alexander. Hilda was invited to the party to perhaps find a rich beau. Could anyone guess that some 40 years after this chance meeting, this blonde would shape my destiny?

2012.

I came into my lonely Manhattan apartment one dark, dismal evening. Now I was 73, it was 2012. I had been widowed for three years. The house Howard and I built, with our family's names carved in the cement foundation, belongs to another family these days. All those stuck-ups have retired in Florida, divorced or died. Their grown children and grandchildren have moved out of the now-Orthodox Five Towns. Connecticut and the North Shore are where they reside.

As I walked into my flat, I checked for phone messages. That's when I heard this:
"Hi Dee, this is Hilda Nieves. I got your number from Dennis Martin. My cousin Mitch is making a reunion of friends from Chester Street. He'd like for you to come. I'm not sure I'll be there as I'm going out town. I might not be back in time." She finished with Mitch's

phone number to RSVP.

I had not seen her cousin Mitch for about 20 years. The rest of the bunch I had not kept up with at all since I was 17 years old. I had married at 18, to a boy from out of Brownsville, and moved away. Thus, none of our paths crossed, except ironically Hilda's and mine. It was by chance since we both today live on the Upper Eastside now, as does Dennis Martin. His wife, Lola is deceased. We'd run into each other occasionally, hug and quip "How are you, take care and goodbye!"

With a glass of pinot in hand to steady myself, I phoned Mitch to RSVP.

"Hello what a nice surprise this is! I'd love to come to the reunion." Then we chatted quite a while as we were old pals who had lost touch with each other. "Dee, it will be held at Dio's Restaurant at 7:30 Tuesday." I was familiar with the Upper East Side eatery. At the end of the call he said, "Someone will be excited you're coming."

"Who's that?" I asked curiously.

"Justin Frank," he answered.

"How nice… With his wife?" I asked.

"No, she died 3 years ago."

Justin had been my last boyfriend before I married my husband. I was taken aback to learn that we were both widowed the same year.

One Week Later.

The night of the reunion arrived. It was a wintery, cold mix of rain and snow. I was nervous the week leading up to the party! I wanted to go, but was terrified of seeing this group after 53 long years, especially Justin. The last they saw me, I was a glamorous girl of 17 in stilettos with long black hair, full of promise. Now I was a woman in her 70's, in black flats. I was attractive for my age, but had lost confidence with my husband's passing. The Chester Street "kids" on the other hand, I imagined they probably looked almost the same, having had plastic surgery, no doubt. Now of course, I was sorry I hadn't done this improvement while I had had the opportunity, but I had chickened out. Meanwhile I drove my best friend Joyce crazy agonizing over what to wear until I resigned to wearing a black soft pantsuit. With my lucky angel silver pin and hammered silver earrings it looked fine, we decided. The pants covered my suede lace-ups. Good thing I was 5'6", I congratulated myself. My long, black mink coat topped with my white silk scarf did the trick, I thought as I glimpsed in my foyer mirror. Then I checked my watch, it was 7:10… Time to leave my apartment.

This being Manhattan on a foul weather night, getting a taxi was impossible. Much to my surprise, I spotted one as a fellow tenant got out of a cab. I dared not hesitate to wait for another at this hour. Immediately I yelled out to the doorman, "Hurry, hurry, Maurice grab it for me!" He did.

Once in the cab, I noticed the unusually empty streets. I was to be early for the reunion, and being the first there was certainly not my wish. Unfortunately, when the driver dropped me off, the terrible weather left me no choice but to enter Dio's Restaurant. The busy maître checked for the Mitch Levin Party, after I waited my turn with the hungry, impatient people in the reservations line.

"No such party listed here tonight, Madam," he said curtly. "Can it be under another name, perhaps?"

"I don't know who else it could be," I answered, perplexed.

When he observed my cane, his snooty demeanor defrosted. Unbelievably for a New York restaurant, the Maître signaled for his associate.

"Sergio, handle my station," he said to him, while he politely offered his arm to escort me down the steep stairway to the bar in the main dining room, which is sunken below street level. "Please wait here. I have your name and party info. As each group checks in, I'll ask if it's your friends." I had been ready in my nervous, humiliated state to go home and forget the whole affair. This sweet gesture made me stay and wait awhile. Being too shy to sit at the bar, instead I sat alone at a high top.

Still in my coat I tried to stay put, but I couldn't! After five minutes I jumped up to ask the hostess to check her book for the same party.

"No such reservation tonight," she said. I was ready to bolt but once again, she suggested I hold her arm while she escorted me through the entire restaurant. Perhaps I'd recognize some familiar faces in the completely booked, cavern-like hall. It was not easy maneuvering between the overflowing tables, for this was a family style restaurant. Waiters tried to move huge platters of hot pizza, pastas, above their sweating heads, while wandering toddlers, parked strollers and highchairs competed for room. Mortified, I didn't see a soul I knew. I was ready to cry like a jilted bride, when she implored me to give it five minutes as it was only 7:40 and the inclement weather might be the problem.

Defeated I allowed the hostess to return me to my perch by the bar. It was there I noted the sudden appearance of a tall, important looking man in a three-piece pinstripe suit. He looked to me like a man of authority in the place. I'll go to the head of the fish instead of its tail, this time, I reasoned to myself as a last resort.

"Can you please help me," I whispered to him, in desperation. He bent down to listen to my tale of woe, and then promptly checked the reservation book. He immediately had a thought.

"Are you sure that you're in the RIGHT Dio's Restaurant?" he asked.

"Is there another?" I stupidly replied. I never bothered to ask Mitch if it wasn't the restaurant in the neighborhood we frequented.

"Yes, let me check their bookings." Sure enough, the reunion party was being held there. Counting me as a no-show, the group was eating their appetizers. "The head of the fish" wasted no time. He had a cab awaiting me to whisk me across the Park, then downtown to the other Dio's.

Once in the taxi, I was so rattled, I opened up to the Cuban driver. He relished my story of this 53-year reunion, but mostly intrigued with me seeing my first love, Justin, again. He became a man on a mission as he wove rapidly through the crowded, wet streets. When we stopped in front of the red neon lit Dio's, my "chariot driver" did a once-in-a-lifetime gesture for an NYC cab driver—he came around to open the door for me with a gracious, exaggerated bow. We both laughed at the whole ridiculous night thus far…

This Dio's Restaurant in the theater district, near Times Square, proved to be more crowded even than the first. With my paisley cane advancing before my feet, I almost screamed to be heard above the noisy downtown mob. "Levin Party, PLEASE!" I shouted to the host. The startled queue parted like the Red Sea for Moses!

Right away the captain guided me to a side exit, thru the lobby of the shabby hotel next door, down a service elevator to the basement level monster-sized dining room. He left me there in an archway foyer that led into the mica-paneled, very loud ballroom. Dazed, I walked into the filled chaotic room of complete strangers, many of them tourists straight off the airplane, probably. Just that disaster-filled moment, a waiter entered the space, shouting at the top of his lungs.
"Is there a Dee-Dee here? I am looking for Dee-Dee." The entire scene of sheer bedlam almost overtook this overwrought 73-year-old!
"M-m-my name is Dee-Dee," I stuttered. With that the waiter pulls from behind his back a hidden bunch of long-stemmed roses, each with dangling handwritten cards.

What is going on here? I thought. Simultaneously I recognize two older faces seated at a large table, to the right of the entry. One face was of Mitch the host, the other Maury Cohen who long ago lived next door to me in Brownsville. He was a vintage version of the toothy, crew-cut boy I now remembered fondly. All the other 20-odd senior citizens I truly did not know on sight.

There remained only one empty chair at this table. As you can understand by the night's ordeal, I almost fell into it. The occupant of the chair touching mine turned directly into my face. His cool blue eyes met my overwhelmed brown eyes. We knew each other instantly!

It was my first love, my first boyfriend, Justin Frank. A bolt shot through me! Here was the silver-haired boy/man I had loved until I was a senior in high school. Justin was still a gorgeous guy to me with his blue bell eyes now behind spectacles, his face lightly lined, the same smile… It was Justin, it was déjà vu, it was surreal. It was an out-of-body-experience, like being dead then coming back into a long-ago time. Come to think of it, it would prove to be just that!

While the roses filled my arms, Justin handed me a greeting card that when opened, played Sam Cooke's "You Send Me". That was our song circa mid-1950. At the same time as an excited little boy anxious to give all his gifts at once, he brought a large envelope that contained black and white photos taken of me and us together in Brownsville, when we were boyfriend and girlfriend. I had glistening eyes… It was so touching, so unexpected.

53 years ago, an 18-year-old Dee-Dee had broken his heart by marrying another 20-year-old, named Howard. I had never planned to do that but a prank by my then

12-year-old kid brother set the wheels of all our fates in motion.

Christmas Break 1958.

I remember it well. It was the last day of school before the Christmas holiday, December 1958. As was my routine, I took the subway home from the High School of Art in Manhattan to my home in Brownsville, Brooklyn. My mother had fixed an early supper for me, as I hurriedly changed from my schoolgirl clothes into a more mature outfit for my salesgirl job at the Rainbow on Pitkin Avenue. I had this job to pay for my art supplies. After my quick stop home, I would take the Rockaway Avenue bus to my job from 6:00 to 10:00 P.M.

After I completed my sales for the evening, I wished all a Merry Christmas. As I clocked-out and left the store, I see Howie Kaplan standing just outside the shop's entrance. It was a surprise to see him there.

"Oh hello Howie, which one of the girls are you waiting for"? I asked.

"I'm waiting for you," he said, in his deep baritone. His intense green eyes locked on me.

"Me?" I asked, scared just seeing the 6'4", 225 pound size of him. And his face looked angry, or so I thought. Uh oh! My making fun of him behind his back has finally gotten back to him, I thought nervously.

"I want to talk to you," he said.

"So, talk," I state, calmly, because I knew my fellow employees are still coming out of the store. I was still safe.

"Not here, I'll drive you home, after we talk in my car," he said.

"I can't go in your car, my parents are expecting me right home," I said abruptly, and I turn to make a beeline for the arriving bus, across the street.

"I called your mother and father, they know I'll bring you home, after a while," he said, trotting after me. What could I do? I followed him to his car, wondering how I could defend myself against this big, strong guy. Maybe I could use one of my stiletto killer high heels, I thought. I had no other means of defense.

We get into his parked car. I turn and say to him, "Well… Talk!"

"Not here!" he said, and drove silently on. I had no clue where he was taking me. My brain was racing, going over what I've said against him and to whom. I recalled that a few days before, I called him Baby Huey and made fun of Rhoda Zinn for dating him. She got mad at me because she thought him cool. Maybe it was her to blame for this frightening encounter. But come to think of it, I was never shy about my dislike of this guy. I should have kept it quiet!

He was a blind date of mine for pizza and a Coke about two years earlier. It was arranged by my best friend at the time, Sheila, and her boyfriend Johnny. Howie was Johnny's friend. I took an instant dislike to him, thinking him obnoxious. A know-it-all with too high of an opinion of himself! I could not wait to cut that evening short.

After the blind date, he walked me to my father's building, with the red Hebrew letters painted on the butcher shop windows. My family and I lived in the second-floor apartment above his small neighborhood business. This was a standard set up in our immigrant community until the late 1950's. As my date Howie and I entered the tenement's door, on Riverdale Avenue, we were in the narrow foyer. It was there that he tried to grab and kiss me.

"NO!" I said, as I pulled away. Then to soften my harsh but heartfelt rejection, I added, "Howie, I like you as a friend."

"I don't need any more friends," he almost shouted as he slammed the door shut and left, pissed off.

That encounter started the feud that went on for years between us. Strangely and to my disgust, Sheila (who dropped Johnny and had a new boyfriend, Sal) remained close friends with Howie. The two of them seemed like brother and sister.

Howie was an only child of Polish immigrants, and she was the change of life baby of divorced Polish parents. She was being raised as an only child since her much older brother was away in the armed services. Sheila's mother was named Sheila too, and was also fond of Howie-boy, as she affectionately called him. He would be at their apartment frequently, as was I. I remember teaching him how to Mamba and do the Cha-Cha in Sheila's parlor. He dated a number of my friends and they liked him. I still would make fun of him behind his back. All knew my dislike of his annoying demeanor, I wasn't shy about it!

Now I was a captive audience in his locked car, and he was deadly mum, as he kept his eyes completely focused in front of him. Finally, he pulled into a White Castle parking lot. My heart pounded in fear.

It was not until he turned and was ready to face me, that I heard the reason why he showed up at the shop, and why my parents who didn't even know him, give him permission to pick me up at work.

Here goes, who could make this story up? The same day my mother accompanied my father on his deliveries of meat orders after the butcher shop closed for the day. They left my bratty 12-year-old brother, Teddy, home alone. The telephone rang and he answered it.

"Dee-Dee?" Howie asked nervously, since Teddy's voice was indistinguishable from mine when he was young.

"Y –yeah, who is this and what do you want?" Teddy replies, the troublemaker smiling, smelling a chance to make mischief.

"It's me, Howard... I saw you at the IRT train station and you looked so good to me. Can I take you out tonight?" Howard asked, emboldened. Teddy can hardly contain himself as he pretended to be me, doesn't know who the hell this shmuck is, and lays it on heavy.

"Oh, Howie I'm so crazy about you.... Of course I'd love to see you tonight," he said, cooingly. All the while he knows full well, I'm working from six to 10, and won't be home. "Let's make at 7:30P.M. Come to my house, sweetie. Do you know where I live?" Howard answers him, puzzled.

"Of course I remember where you live on Riverdale. You are the Butcher's Daughter." My claim to fame!

Later that day my parents return home. The family ate dinner together. Teddy told them nothing about what he's been up to. Suddenly at 7:30 there's somebody knocks at the apartment door.

"Who's there?" my father asks. My father opens the door to see a stranger who is a very tall, well-dressed young man.

"Hello, I'm Howard Kaplan, I'm here to take Dee-Dee out." My father looks at him.

"You must be mistaken. She is not home." He is about to shut the door when Howard protests, "But Mr. Diamond, I called her earlier this evening, and we made the date together."

Meanwhile, my roly-poly brat of a brother is rolling with laughter, to think he made this date and the guy actually showed up! Both my parents and Howard were embarrassed at Teddy's mean prank. They liked the boy, felt his disappointment and told him where I worked and what time to pick me up. Since this was before cell phones, nobody bothered to be in touch with me at the store tell me about it.

While I was relieved that he wasn't going to hurt me in any way, I was smoldering mad that that rotten brat had put me in this position. I would NEVER go out with Howie then, I was worried that someone who knew me would see me with him, especially Justin my boyfriend, who shared with me a young, intense first love.

This fellow, Mr. Kaplan, who I had avoided on the subway, (like if I saw him in one train car, I'd be sure to sit in another one) had me here alone. We lived two train stations away from each other. He was going to college, while I was still in high school in Manhattan. We took the same train at the same time. If he caught up with me, I'd get an earful of his being the social director of his fraternity, and a superior older man while I was "still a baby" in high school. Oh, how I hated him!

Far from home, in Howie's car I was forced to hear him out and look at the 19-year-old man he had become. I reluctantly admired his plans for the future to become a construction engineer. While studying, he had a great job where the boss was molding him into a British textile designer. His boss promised that he would treat him as a son, if he would stay at his company.

We were both ambitious, artistic kids and first-generation Americans. Our dream was to achieve success and get out of Brooklyn. Ironically, today that's where the young want to move, into Brooklyn.

Now he seemed to have a more confidence and a less belligerent air about him. He had lost the tough guy big shot 'hood of East New York along with the black motorcycle/boots and DA hair persona. Now he wore an English tweed sport jacket, a button-down shirt and a clean-cut haircut. I was pleasantly impressed, but I didn't want to be in his company. That was Tuesday night, December 23, 1958.

Howard, for he didn't want to be called Howie anymore, ask me out for that Saturday night. I said I was busy. Same for that Friday, and Thursday, but he wouldn't let up so reluctantly. I gave in to just get rid of him, I would go out with him the following night, Wednesday. I planned on going out of our area so no one would see us. There was no reason to tell Justin since I never imagined dating him again. My rotten brother would really get it this time! I swear my parents kept him out of my sight for a month.

I saw Howard Wednesday, then he talked me into Thursday, by Friday he pinned me with his fraternity pin. Talk about giving me the grand rush, he then gave me a Star of David, with a heart designed on it, then a friendship ring, he literally spun me around. I didn't say a word to anyone, especially Justin, who for some reason was not around that week.

That Saturday night I made plans with Sheila and Sal to go out with my new mystery man and me. Sheila guessed every possible guy I or she ever dated (we knew each other since kindergarten), but never brought up Howard's name because that was completely out of the realm of possibility. When Howard and I knocked at Sheila's apartment door, she, Carl, and Sheila, Sr. screamed in unison.

"NO NO no Howie! No-o it can't be Howie." I can almost hear their screams of disbelief to this day.

Now Justin must be told about my change of heart, I worried. I felt very bad, but I was caught in a triangle. Justin and I had been going together for a while, but we were both too shy to say "I love you". Howard was determined to marry me. My parents and extended family preferred him for me. I was confused and involved in high school graduation, selecting a college and my mother informing me that I would have to work during the day and go to college at night. Thus F.I.T. would fit the bill, as Howard had decided to stay with British Textiles, and we could go to night school while we both held jobs. Then his parents bought a large house in Rockaway for us. His parents saw me as the daughter they always wanted

Justin was caught off guard. He wasn't in a position to entertain marriage at the time, but he silently thought it was going to happen for us, because we belonged together.

One day he chances an impromptu meeting with me face to face. He comes up to my apartment above the butcher shop, with a loving card in hand. He holds me and professes his love. He gently kisses me on my eyelids and realizes I'm not his girl anymore. I am moved to almost tears when he is leaving, as I heard Howard coming up the hallway staircase. Howard is angry and bellows at Justin.
"If I ever see you here again… I'll kill you!" Howard shouted, glaring at him. I see Justin's shoulders droop as he departs, defeated.

Although he lived across the street, I only saw him once more by accident, as we board the same train car going to work in the morning rush hour. It was about 4 months after our sad parting. I am sporting a new sparkling engagement ring. Justin is standing in front of me making polite impersonal conversation with me, when a man who was seated next to me gets up and says to Justin, "Please take my seat, young man, and sit next to your fiancée." We both said thank you without correcting him. It was too hard to explain.

I married Howard the same year, 1959, and moved away.

Dio's Restaurant, 2012.

Fast forward to the Chester Street reunion at Dio's Restaurant in 2012. We are so happy to meet once again. We both have lived through long marriages, the illnesses and cancer deaths of our spouses, who were in the same hospital and died the same year.

We've taken our time to get to know how we feel about our bond of love that seems unbroken. Guilt has been a factor we discuss because of our happiness and the sad departure of our respective spouses. He and I are sensitive to our adult children realizing we are each others' "first and last love". It is important for them to know we loved our respective spouses and there was no contact between us.

It is a poignant fact of this late-in-life love that when we are together, we are familiar even though we were apart more than a half century. I see flashes of the boy I loved at 16 in the man I love at 75. He says he too sees me the same way. I tell him as I affectionately stroke his white hair, that I remember when his hair was dirty blonde as I stroked it a lifetime ago.

It's just in time now, for the Butcher's Daughter and her Justin from Chester Street.

A Sunday in Papa's Automobile

At noon on Sunday morning we heard keys opening our apartment door. In would come Papa, with bags brimming with Sunda's special breakfast. I don't think we called it brunch yet. Bagels, lox, chubs (we kids called it goldfish), sturgeon, baked salmon, and pickled herring. And of course, cream cheese. Then out of the refrigerator would appear thin sliced tomatoes and onions, topped with black glistening olives.

Oh boy, did we feast! Was it a wonder we were never a svelte clan! After such a gorging, Sam Diamond, his wife, Rose, my older sister Sissy, my younger, bratty brother Teddy and I set out for the day's next entertainment. We would race each other to get whatever we thought was the best seat, in the back of our cramped 1937 Buick. It was then the bickering would begin.

None of us liked what we got, and certainly not each other. The old car took a while to warm up. Without any mechanical finesse, my father would tear the gears brutally, and off we'd go with a jolt. He'd whip the automobile up to 20 mph. If he'd accidentally accelerate to 21mph, my mother would give a shout.
"Sam, you're speeding!" she'd say, shrilly.
"Be quiet, schlock," he would answer back. All this time we in the back we bicker continuously. We'd spot a red light, and all this car's occupants would brace for what laid ahead. For it was my father's habit (being the smooth operator he was), to accelerate his car to the light, then slam on the brakes. All of us would then be thrown forward, then back, fast. We all had black and blue marks and bumped heads throughout our childhood.

Let me say bluntly Papa had no sense of direction. Stubbornly, he made a point to never ask for directions, because he always thought he knew where he was going!

On this Sunday he created, as usual, havoc on the highway traffic. The family was en route to Highland Park, in Brooklyn. As always, he wove dangerously in and out of lanes. The fast lane, where he certainly didn't belong, was his choice venue. Wandering over the lines was how he navigated. He was oblivious to the horns of his fellow drivers. Abruptly from the fast lane, my father, without signals to the other cars (or us), turned sharply off the highway.

"Sam, where are you going? I don't remember going to the park this way!" my mother shouts to her husband.
"Schlock be quiet!" he yells. "It's a shortcut!"
"Looks like a sidewalk to me," she shoots back. This doesn't stop him from continuing his set course. It was difficult to believe this normally tranquil man could turn into such a tyrant. All it took was the power of his automobile key to crown him "King of The Road"!

There was silence from the back of the Buick, even we stopped baiting and poking and pinching each other. The dialogue from the front sounded scary, even to us. Remember this driver only looked like our Papa, but didn't act like him.

.

Loaded with confidence, he continued on his chosen path, even as it grew narrower and narrower. He only stopped the car when it got stuck. By this time my mother was fainting. This was the situation. The roundish hump of 1937 model Buick, filled with a screaming frantic family, was wedged against a chain link fence surrounding a reservoir. Beside us was a steep ravine leading to the six-lane fast moving highway.

"The children! The children! We'll all drown!" my mother wailed helplessly.

Her husband was no longer so sure of himself. The prevailing sentiment from the back was that we were really in trouble this time! The fact that Mama started crying and Papa was NOT yelling "shlock be quiet!" seemed to do it. The obvious absence of anyone nearby to witness or rescue us further added to our distress.

Then my mother trembled as she commanded, "Do not shake the car, do not shake the car!" It must have been an hour, when a reservoir guard, on routine foot patrol, spotted our car blocking his path.

"B-B-But how, or why did you get here?" the guard asked, taking off his uniform hat and scratching his shocked head. From the backseat of the teetering Buick we tattle-tails sobbed vehemently,

"Papa was taking one of his short cuts, Mom told him to turn back, but he wouldn't listen!"

It took a radioed police tow to very delicately pry the Diamonds and their vehicle free. Another lovely Sunday afternoon drive… But this time we made the Daily News!

The Disruptor

1948. It was the year of the disruption, dislocation, redecorating, anticipation, and beginning of a lifelong addiction.

Our apartment on Stone Avenue, in Brownsville, Brooklyn, was to live through its revolution to modernity. Its status quo turned upside down and right side up to accommodate our new star border. This was no small feat since there was no extra space to maneuver.

My parents were forced to move their bedroom, with its bulky furniture, into their two daughters' much smaller former bedroom. The little girls had to leave their brown iron beds, relics from their own mother's childhood. Even their beloved wooden radio with its goldish dial was carried off somewhere.

We sisters were moved into our father and mother's larger bedroom. Now we were to sleep on the brand-new sofa bed. It would be opened at night to become our beds. During the day it would be dressed with a burgundy slip cover, piped in forest green. Bolsters and throw pillows were arranged against the wall it paralleled. A pair of end tables with lamps appeared suddenly, too.

Above the sofa was hung a large round mirror, stylish and unframed. Two armchairs touching on another wall were bought for additional seating. They were slip-covered too, in forest green, and piped in burgundy.

Facing the sofa was my parents' high chest of drawers where we girls shared the drawer space. New floral drapes framed the room's two windows with burgundy, beige and greens. With the dark forest walls the print of the drapes and pillows we kvelled. No doubt my mother had been influenced by some movie set she had seen, probably in the Loewe's Pitkin Theatre.

When you entered the newly-named living room (nee Mommy and Papa's bedroom), through the single glass pane door, all eyes were drawn to the piece de résistance, the reason for the upheaval, for the freshly painted walls, for the new furniture, or as my father called it, "the pogrom".

It was the arrival of our first television set, the star of our shabby, not quite chic apartment. It was called the "Capart" console 14-inch television, with doors. To think that because of it, we got a special new living room magically carved out of the same square footage of our walk-up quarters!

Imagine the world of entertainment that then beamed into our new oasis, in dreary Brownsville from that miracle called... television! Our family's life was forever changed.

Stone Cookies from Stone Avenue

This story is about quality over quantity, never wasting food, and how I learned salesmanship from Rose Diamond, my mother.

As usual my mother was overwhelmed on one Friday before the Sabbath. Per her routine, early in the morning she would grind the fish for gefilte fish. Then she would mix it with eggs, matzah meal, onion, salt and pepper, then gently roll it into even balls. They would be plopped into the waiting simmering broth she had made from the fish bones, onions, carrots, celery, parsley, salt and pepper, adding a pinch of sugar too.

While that pot was cooking my mother would take the chicken she already oshered, rinsed to first use for soup, then half-cooked it would be removed, covered with spices, stuffed, surrounded by vegetables, then roasted. She'd then fry its fat and extra skin with more onions, and its liver while eggs were hard boiled to be combined then chopped in a wooden bowl, to make what else? Chopped liver. Later she would cut up the salad vegetables and set the Sabbath table.

It was time now for her to bake for the weekend. On the enamel-topped kitchen table, she dumped a mound of flour straight from the Heckler's sack. A well was dug in the center, eggs broken into it, and oil and water were thrown in in an unmeasured manner. She absentmindedly added sugar and salt along with a fistful of poppy seeds. This she rolled it all into a huge speckled ball. Without rest, the dough was rolled into a big slab, cut with a juice glass into rounds then baked. When light tan they were taken out of the busy single oven to cool.

After all the food was cooked and the baking done, then Mom would mop the linoleum floors of our apartment. Carefully, she covered the still-damp surface with sheets of old newspaper. This was to keep them from soil when we kids would run in from the street after school. This was a common practice for mothers to employ before the Sabbath in the Stone Avenue tenements where we lived.

I was first to arrive home from school that Friday. Our home was filled with such delicious, familiar smells. While I tiptoed from one newspaper sheet to the next, I sneaked a poppy seed cookie into my hungry mouth. When I bit into it, I almost cracked my baby teeth on it.

"Mommy, the cookie was hard as a rock!" I cried, as I handed it to her. She bit into my same cookie cautiously. It dawned on her then that in her haste she had forgotten to put in baking powder in the dough.

My mother's imagination quickly spun a fairy tale to sell her failed batch of poppy seed cookies.
"Oh," she explained, smiling, "But honey these are magic stone cookies. They are meant to be dunked in milk or Sabbath tea, then and only then, will they turn soft and delicious to the special person eating them."

A glass of milk was poured for me at the kitchen table. I timidly took a "stone cookie", dunked it into the milk, and magic happened! I loved the stone cookie. It was soft, sweet and crunchy, with the little poppy seeds peppered through. Our whole family loved the "Magic Stone Cookies", so she had to make them for us again and again.

A Rose by Any Other Name

Roses, roses were in decadent bloom.

More than a few females in my family of that last
generation were named for this lovely flower. This was
a family fact and dealt with as such.

None were called just plain-old Rose. As we were an
immigrant clan with "a bouquet of Roses", we added
unique character descriptions to each.

There was "Zaftig Rose", "Bag of Bones Rosie",
"Yonker's Rose", "Moonie's Rose" and our Italian
Rose, "Rowe". The Rose I'll be telling you about is
"Shtuma Rosie". Shtum in Yiddish means quiet and
indeed this Rosie was, in deepest affection, the quiet
one. She was born mute.

Shtuma Rosie and my mother, "Zaftig Rose", were first
cousins. They were contemporaries and very close.
Each lived with their husbands and children in
Brooklyn. One lived in Williamsburg, the other a
distant subway ride away in Brownsville. It was a joyful
reunion whenever my mother's dear cousin visited.
They each had so much to catch-up on. Siblings, in-
laws, out-laws, who was fighting, who was expecting,
who was having an affair, who had health or money
problems.

These talkative Roses had so much to gossip about, but
they had a major problem. One Rosie could not speak,
nor was she taught to read lips. Alas, my mother could
not sign. What to do, what to do?

It was my father, "Sammy the Butcher", who came up

with the perfect solution. While stacking a delivery of large brown paper bags in his kosher butcher shop, he got an idea.

He took out a large pair of shears, cut the bags wide open and brought the entire stack home. With a handful of pens he said graciously, "Roses, now you can talk your hearts out!" These two short-stemmed Roses, now armed with these tools, commenced mad venting at our enamel/metal kitchen table.

So, how's your Saul and the children? My mother would begin, in her slanted, flowing handwriting. Her cousin would then answer, in her small, tight hand.
They're all OK, thank G-d, except for Louie who has the Gripe. He probably got it from that skinny girlfriend of his, Pauline. She doesn't wear a sweater even if its chilly outside! Shtuma Rosie wrote back.

On and on, the Roses would scribble furiously all afternoon. They would make the accompanying grimaces and smiles to animate the brown paper bag script. There were chuckles and tears. Mostly the sounds in the warm tenement kitchen was of their pens scratching on the stiff leaves of paper.

I can see myself as a young, pigtailed girl, skipping home from school, pushing our apartment door open, and knowing at once who was visiting. I had to watch my step so as not to trip over the clutter of used brown paper, floating on the waxed linoleum floor, as I ran to kiss both Roses. When evening grew near, my mother, Zaftig Rose, hugged her cousin Rosie. She loaded her with noshes for the long ride home, in a brown paper bag.

Joe, Our Comic Book Hero

"Is he there yet?" us kiddies would ask, every few minutes for we were so anxious. When word that "Joe the Comic Book Man" was indeed coming to the cement Brownsville playground, we children would flock there. He was our Pied Piper.

Carefully, he would untie the knotted rope bundles of treasure to make piles of the used comic books of every genre. We, the kids of poor immigrants, could never afford to own new comics, even at 10 cents each from the candy store on the corner. Almost every other corner had a candy store in those days.

We could take one of our choosing at a time, grab a seat on a park bench near Joe, read it, return it to its pile respectfully, then start on another and another. For many of us, this is how we learned to love reading, starting with just the colorful pictures first.

Our parents approved of Joe. It was rumored that he was a lonely bachelor from somewhere in the neighborhood who loved to make kids happy. He was a garbageman by trade, and he saved any comics he could salvage to bring this magical library to us lucky kids.

The Star at Mrs. Diamond's Sabbath Table

Real magic was what my late, thrifty mother would do to a chicken come the Sabbath dinner.

This performance was the ritual every Friday throughout my Brownsville childhood. I am 76 years old now but still marvel at her technique.

1. She'd do liposuction on the bird, extracting all the blobs of yellow, shining fat she'd find under its white/pink skin.

2. Any loose skin was surgically severed, then snipped into small pieces. Now together with the fat, this skin and chunks of yellow onions were rendered into schmaltz (chicken fat) and gribenes (cracklings). The chicken fat was used generously all the following week to fry and flavor food. The cracklings were scrumptious on a thick slab of seeded rye bread or challah.

3. The simmering red liver would be sautéed to a pinkish-brown, with a another batch of diced onions (in schmaltz of course). In Bubbie's round, worn wooden bowl, it is chopped finely with hardboiled eggs. The half-moon shaped steel chopper hitting this bowl, is a distinct recurring sound of my childhood. This became a mound of deliciousness, served as an appetizer when she offered it on a bed of lettuce, tomato and green pepper circles.

4. The next use of this fowl was to have its feet, neck bone, pupick and entire body plopped into a big pot of water, perfumed with fresh dill, parsley, parsnip, celery, carrots and a whole round onion. About 30 minutes hence, the partially cooked pale whole chicken and its

loose parts were scooped out of this jacuzzi. This broth would be called "Chicken Noodle Soup" or "Matzah Ball Soup" depending on whatever Mom would later top it with.

5. Further use of the manipulated wings, feet, neck bone, were employed by throwing them into an awaiting crock of bubbling sweet and sour tomato sauce with tiny meatballs. This was my mother's fricassee, or called appetizer #2, to be sopped up with the soft belly of the challah. My mouth still waters remembering this savory dish.

6. Not to be overlooked, was the empty sock of the skin of the neck. It would be filled to bursting with a mixture of matzah meal, grated carrot, onion, minced garlic and moistened with, you guessed it, schmaltz. It was then sewn closed with ordinary white thread at both open ends. A skilled plastic surgeon couldn't have done a better job! This, now called "helzelah", would be cuddled next to and baked in the same roasting pan as the hen.

Also, a ring of white potatoes and medallions of carrots hugged this crowded space. But before being pushed into the oven, it had to be smeared with Mama's special paste of catsup, a little oil, garlic powder, pepper and paprika.

This coating was the secret to produce the shiny, well-tanned, movie star of a Sabbath chicken.

The Shoe-House Block

Once upon a time, before shoes had red painted soles, and cost a literal fortune, there was a magical place called "The Shoe-House Block". It was on Pebble Avenue, between Loverdale Avenue and Lowport Street circa 1940's-1950's.

After the essential corner candy store, the entire Brownsville block was attached two-family shingled houses with steps climbing up to wooden porches. Over each porch swung a metal sign of a large black shoe.

Every first floor contained bare windows, through which from the street one could see into the brightly lit shop. There were shelves floor to ceiling of endless boxes of shoes. The rest of the inventory was down in the basement. The owner/shopkeeper lived in the rear of shop with his family.

On the second floor lived a family of renters. This was the set-up of the row of dwellings known by the neighborhood as the Shoe-House Block.

Entire families would purchase their shoes there, season after season. Feet both small and narrow, large and wide, would be fitted carefully. Babies would have their chubby, tiny feet held flat on the metal measuring piece by the shoe expert, as they were fitted for their first pair. The beaming parents trusted the patient shopkeeper for this milestone in their lives.

For us children he would leave extra room for growth, as much as possible, since he understood our immigrant parents couldn't buy shoes frequently.

Before each sale was rung up, he would ask, "Would you like taps on the heels and toes of the shoes for about a dollar more?"

"Yes, please", the adults would always answer, for this would make the shoes last longer. Remember that we walked, or skated, or jumped rope, or played ball on the rough cement sidewalks of Brooklyn. Even with taps on our shoes, sometimes we had to use cardboard inside our worn-out shoes to cover holes in their soles, until we could get new ones.

For the summer we girls would get sandals white or red. In winter, laced oxfords. I have a sweet memory of my immaculate, polished white sandals as I skipped home from P.S. 184 for lunch, one ordinary sunny June day. I was about 8 and the school was on the next block. My feet felt so good in my sandals, so happy to know I didn't have to wear my heavy brown oxfords… It really was summer!

Carol's "A"

I wasn't there, but I've heard this family story a hundred times.

Carol was one of Auntie Esther's 20-plus grandchildren. She was visiting her grandmother, who was my mother Rose's older sister. The two elderly sisters, Esther and Rose, were always close and lived near each other in Brownsville.

Now in their later years, they lived in Miami Beach, only a few blocks apart. Carol is my mother's great niece from Maryland, and she called to say she's in town. She wants to see Aunt Rose while she's here, too. My mother drops whatever she's doing and rushes over.

When my mother walks into her sister's apartment on art deco Collins Avenue, the tea kettle is softly whistling, awaiting her to have a cup of tea with them. Carol's tea bag is slightly ripped open. She is anxious for her great Aunt to read her tea leaves. The entire family thinks she has the "gift".

At first, my mother plays the familiar game denying she can. "Carol, dear I really can't read tea leaves", she responds, coyly.
"Please give it a try… For fun, Auntie Rose," she pleads, so sweetly. Then the great Aunt says the classic, "I'll see… I'll see," while pretending to ponder, which really means, "Yes, of course, but if I can't remember, you forced me." This is our family hieroglyphics we all clearly read.

In the meantime, they chat and polish off Auntie Esther's china dish of homemade rugelach. Soon my mother instructs her niece to spin her emptied cup three times to dissipate any liquid so there won't be any tears.

The 30-year-old Carol does what she's told reverently. She watches as her cup is tilted this way, then that way, with controlled drama by Rose before she stuns her audience of two.
"Who is "A"?" she questions, raising her black arched eyebrows. "He's gonna be your husband, and soon, Carol. This Mr. A is a tall one and has light hair" she adds now with conviction. Carol, who was considered almost an "old maid", couldn't believe what she was just told.

Auntie Rose could not possibly know her great niece was serious with this guy, named Arthur. He was purchasing her engagement ring while she was in Miami. They had secretly planned for their wedding day, before she left to tell her grandma in person, that this old maid of the clan was finally getting married. My mother, the tea leaf reader, unintentionally stole her surprise!

It became added proof to the family lore that Auntie Rose knew her tea leaves, alright!

Bread

Bread was such important part of my Brownsville childhood. We ate bread at every meal, except on Passover.

Whole dense loaves of bread were bought by my father at dawn, from the cooperative bakery somewhere in Brownsville. Our breakfast on schooldays was usually a thick slab of pumpernickel, rye or Eastern European cornbread. On it was layered butter, or farmer cheese or jelly, or all the above. We drank milk-based coffee or tea with milk with it.

Winter lunchtime, when we walked home from school, would be some hot milk-based soup… Like potato, corn or tomato, all started from Campbell's cans, with bread and butter. But in the hot weather, it would be cold refreshing beet borscht, schav, dandelion, or spinach soup (dolloped with sour cream) & diced cucumber. Of course, hunks of bread and butter were the staple accompaniment.

For variety we had thick-sliced sandwiches with tuna fish, salmon salad or American cheese. My mother would generously coat the bread with Hellman's mayonnaise, then finish them with lettuce and tomato squashed in.

Dinner was salad with bread on the side. Then, a main course of some meat or a fish dish with a starch of some sort, and overcooked vegetables, 50's style. We were encouraged throughout the meal by my mother, "Eat bread or you'll be hungry later!"

If we ate herring or fish, hard crusts of bread were kept at the ready if a tiny bone perchance got stuck in our throats. We kids were instructed by my father, "Push it down by roughly chewing, then swallowing the bread."

On the Sabbath we ate the best bread of all: challah, with its amber-braided shiny crust and soft pale-yellow interior, so perfect for sopping gravy and adding joy to the festive Friday night meal. Any crumbs from this bread we fed to the birds. My father called them golden crumbs.

Saturday afternoon was spent at the movie theater. This was an all-day event. My sister Sissy and I were loaded with two challah chicken sandwiches, in a brown lunch bag, to sustain us for the day at the movies.

We knew it was Sunday morning because we had another kind of bread on the table: bagels, meant for piling on cream cheese and lox.

I recall once being in my father's old car with him at the wheel, mother seated next to him, my boyfriend, Howie and myself in the backseat. We were on the Long Island expressway on the way to visit Hempstead State Park, when my mother turns around to hand Howie a huge American cheese sandwich in wax paper, on thick-sliced rye bread. She knew that was his favorite. Howie smiled at this obvious sweet gesture. I, however, was mortified!

In this case the bread was used as bait… To capture me my husband!

You Can Take the Girl Out of Brooklyn...

Strolling one sunny afternoon, I spot a new tiny boutique on Madison Avenue. It sells handcrafted home gifts. Killing time now that I'm retired, I wander in.

The packed cluttered shop is empty. Then I hear a lone woman chatting on a phone in its rear. The shopkeeper has her back to me. Would you believe that by her body I know who she is?

"Tootsie Travitz!" I scream out impulsively. She drops the phone and turns around like a caught fugitive in her quiet store. The middle-aged grandmother is shaken to be called by her maiden name, Travitz. I see her shocked face and yell out, "I'm Dee-Dee Diamond from Stone Avenue, the Butcher's Daughter. I was a playmate of your sister, Aliza."

Tootsie was taken aback to say the least, because this was about 50 years ago. I think she didn't exactly remember me until she really stared deeply into my face and I mentioned her parents' kosher delicatessen that had been on a corner, near Baby Swing Park in Brownsville.

Then her eyes glazed over, and we hugged hello and caught up on the few people we still heard from. I bought some tchotchke just to be nice, and then we bid one other a fond "See ya and call me."

How did I know that she was Mrs. Travitz' daughter, you ask? I couldn't tell her, but her appearance was like a ghost of my past. Tootsie had the exact build of her late mother. That made my mouth water, imagining once more the frankfurters, mustard, sauerkraut and knishes I ate in her parents' restaurant so many years ago, in the 40's and 50's. To our neighborhood, this was the ultimate cuisine of deliciousness!

Mr. and Mrs. Travitz ran the place together. Her father was almost a blur to me now, except he was a red-haired, smiley counterman. Their mother, however, is clearly etched in my childhood's eye.

She was heavy-set, waist-less square, with spindly bird-like legs. Mrs. Travitz had to wear her large white apron tied just over her ample bosom. I often pondered while munching on my potato knish (split and slathered with yellow mustard), how her delicate thin legs held her up while she ran from the counter to tables to serve customers. Those legs did not look like they belonged to her, but to some other skinny mommy, or a stork.

My family and I moved out of the neighborhood years ago. I cannot recall ever seeing or thinking of the Travitz Delicatessen or their family since. Now as fate would play it, I encounter this DNA clone of Mrs. Travitz in this boutique, and I'm a kid again... Salivating for a frankfurter, and potato knish.

Buzzie of the Boys

We ten animated ancient boys floated back together, to our mental schoolyard. For a brief evening, we'd forget we were has-beens.

"The Chester Street Boyz" were once more!

This was a reunion of "The Kidz" of Chester Street, Brownsville, in October 2013. I was the "Baby" of the pals, at 72. It was held at Alexio's Restaurant, a few blocks from where I live now in Manhattan. Unfortunately, its location constituted a safari for most of these alte kakers. We hadn't seen each other in unison for 55 years. I pondered just how long it had been since any of them ventured even a few blocks out of their present, familiar neighborhoods.

Louie and Murray came from Staten Island. It meant a ferry ride with train changes. Some, like Tony and Arnie, ventured from distant, blue-collar suburban New Jersey towns. Stewie, Harvey and Donny schlepped from upstate New York. They chipped in to pay for parking next to the restaurant. A trio took a bus from Queens. One bravely endured the dreary subway from Brooklyn. A tough old geezer he was, and proud of it!

After shocked recognition and embraces, we were seated in a private party room. Lots of shouted "What, what?" echoed, and repeated, at our long dinner table. We were the original generation of Rock 'n Rollers, circa 1950's. Thus, most of us were deaf— in only in one ear, if lucky.

Bifocaled eyes roamed the Italian menu for soft, easy -to-chew and -digest dishes. No spicy or fried things would do for our "Road Warriors". It goes without saying, they heeded their weak kidneys and did not drink too much, or else. Still, the men's room was frequented numerous times... But who was counting!

Laughter with squeals of delight accompanied each exaggerated tale from our distant past. Funny, a few couldn't name any current events, but boy oh boy could they remember the "bad girls" they had sloppy sexual encounters with more than a half century ago.

Muriel, a then older married, horny woman of yesteryear, whose name caused a bellowing outburst of "Where's Muriel now?"
"She's probably screwing some corpses in her mausoleum!"

The frail, most probably asexual buddies were once again hormone hopping hunks, if only in their foggy minds. You can believe me, we had a few nearly choking emergencies, following each funny or silly boyish recollection. Whacks on the backs got stuck morsels of food dislodged, then shooting 'cross the table.

My folks had labelled these boys, "Hoodlums, good-for-nothings." These were the ones that hang out at the corner McCreed's Candy Store, or Katz's Pool Hall above the pharmacy across the street. They cut school, smoked looseys, played poker and went to the track. Whistling and cat-calling followed any girl passing who caught the Boyz' eye.

A popular song that would blast from the candy store jukebox was "Standing on the Corner Watching all the Girls go by". This seemed our 1950's theme song. We Boyz snuck into the neighborhood movies, and fought with kids from other streets. In between, we boxed at the Brownsville Boys' Club. Often, we played stickball in the P.S. 184 cement school yard… Or right on the block.

Let me tell you how the Boyz got even—with tricks pulled on neighbors we didn't like. How we youngsters, party to their pranks snickered and repressed giggles, while with disguised voices they had orders of chickens, meat, and produce sent to unsuspecting adults. The old people who they had annoyed called the police, or threw pots of hot water on them, then chased them home late at night. How dare they need their relief from our constant ball playing, singing, fighting and the general uproar we caused on the block? The phone calls were made from a public booth on the corner. Then the raggedy gang of trouble makers would hide to watch how the recipient of the unwanted parcels argued with the delivery man, "I didn't order it, and I won't pay for it… Get the hell out of here!" the old people would scream in Yiddish/Brooklynese.

Why we thought this was so comical, you'd have to be there. We old fuddy-duddies smacked our bony knees. Weren't we the cutest!

Swimming in the neighborhood, chlorine-reeking pool each summer was nirvana to them. Some didn't even like using the bathtubs in their shabby "toilets" at home. Of course, they all forgot that fact. We learned to swim without instruction, by throwing each other dangerously in the deep crowded, pool called Betsy Head Park.

We Boyz learnt to dive off the high diving board by daring each other. No one wanted to be called "chicken"! Believe me, the frantic lifeguards were constantly blowing their whistles, to try bringing order to our pack of out-of-control teenagers.

Come to think of it, we were always out on the streets where we invented our own fun. The kids of Brownsville of those days had no reason to stay in our cramped, overcrowded tenements. Some guys escaped from their quarreling, overworked parents and ranting, squabbling or irritating siblings. We were ordered to go play in the street. Our parents needed privacy, space. Quiet! For a few guys, the Boyz were more their family than their biological kin.

On Chester Street, stickball was played with an abandoned broom handle used in place of a bat. "Potsy" was a worn rubber heel, rescued from Boris' Shoe-Repair Shop trash, used as a puck the girls would kick, while hopping from one chalked box to another.

These games were even played at night, under the yellow street lights. Hit the penny and marbles, and some games of skill with flicked soda bottle caps were all going on somewhere on Chester Street. The younger girls played "Boys, Girls" where they simultaneously called out names while they skipped and bounced a pink rubber ball.

A! My Name Is… B! My Name is…etc., until they got to Z. Jump rope and double dutch could be managed with a worn, long cord from a mom's laundry line.

When the winter snow covered the cracked sidewalks, it was battle time. Snow forts were built, artillery of snowballs formed, and then it was all out war. One side of Chester Street against the other. Passing pedestrians were moving targets, as well.

All this was usually the entertainment for the homebound folks resting on their elbows, at their windows, facing this living stage of youthful activity. Truth be known, I hardly remembered these senior citizens.

I moved out of their Mecca, Brownsville, when I was 16. I never looked back till this re-union (thanks Facebook)! A few of the gang were absent. Names I had long-forgotten like the Beaverly boy, Juggio, Groundman, Bad-Bad Buzzie, Hutch, the Polack… Dead or alive were not left unscathed by us "Denture Dandies".

I seated myself next to Maury, the shy guy, who had been my next-door neighbor on Chester Street. We sat at the opposite end of the long dinner table. He and I spoke quietly about our lives in contrast to the rest of the diners. We were however being jolted time after time, with shouting, banging on the table and with booming enthusiastic, breathless howling. Maury and I rolled our eyes at the shenanigans. The Boyz" were milking their adolescence, perhaps as for its final hurrah.

Through the din, I heard a familiar "Bad-Bad Buzzie" name brought -up.
"Bad-Bad Buzzie died," I blurted impulsively. "A Facebook friend thought he had heard the rumor," I explained.
"I'm Bad-Bad Buzzie and I think I'm alive," there came a shout from a slightly bent, frizzy-haloed chap at the other end of the long table. Embarrassed I then realized the chubby, hilarious Bad-Bad Buzzie of faded memory.

My crotchety cronies, Bad-Bad Buzzie, and even I, roared with hoarse laughter at my expense. After my faux pas, every few minutes someone yelled out, "Where's "The Buzz"… Is he dead?"

And he'd holler back, "I'm NOT dead!!! I'm NOT dead!!!" as he would make an exaggerated gesture of pinching to reassure himself... You see, Bad-Bad Buzzie was still hilarious.

It was about 8:00 P.M. when it was time for us Boyz to give our farewells for our wonderful Chester Street Reunion.

We promised to keep in touch, and not wait another 50 years…

The Antique

The mystery remains—where did the antique come from? How or why did it end up in our humble kitchen in Brownsville, Brooklyn?

Everyone in our family called it the antique. What an elegant eyesore it was! Dark and tall and ornate. It truly had us outclassed.

The antique was a majestic china cabinet that reeked of opulence, with its intricate wooden exterior of carved curlicues that lead to a crown of tangled scrolls. The front door, with a lock, was of clear beveled glass. Four baroque legs supported the piece. Faded, once-scarlet velvet covered its interior and shelves. Clusters of an odd assortment of bric-a-brac rested on its shelves. A scattering of carnival glass, cranberry glass wine glasses (etched in gold), a few heart-shaped cut-glass goblets and fruit enameled dessert plates. In this potpourri was a set of Japanese-decorated dishes brought back from overseas, by a marine merchant cousin.

All these pieces were treasured by my mother, so that the antique was kept locked. It stood on the wall between my younger brother's bedroom door and the kitchen window, facing the clothesline where my mother hung out the family wash. It only competed for dominance, in the tenement's pea-green kitchen, with the bulky refrigerator. The other parts of the room were incidental, like table and chairs, a small stove and sink.

All that we children knew, was that it had been Bubbe Clara's, our maternal grandmother from Odessa.

One evening, without a groan, without a moan, the antique gave up! It tried to commit suicide. It couldn't take it anymore in the Diamond's kitchen. So, on that night in the 1940's, the top shelf fell onto the second shelf, which collapsed at an angle onto the bottom shelf. This pogrom crashed all the goblets but one. Most of the post-WWII Japanese china set met its demise, too.

What a CATASTROPHE! I remember the racket it caused... My mother's tears, her screams. We had been enjoying our chicken-fat-fried cutlets, with mounds of creamy mashed potatoes, when the antique imploded. So forceful, like a bomb went off.

Papa tried to calm my hysterical mother down by saying, "Rosie, it was just an old piece of junk, anyway!" Talk about saying the wrong thing! We kids jumped with anxiety.

Well... That caused such a tearful, howling response from his wife, that he had to promise he would get the antique fixed. My mother's first cousin, Rose Merlis' husband, Saul, was a carpenter. So, Saul was called to the antique's rescue. Realistically, there was a problem in using Saul. You see, Saul was deaf, and we lived in a tenement building, that was to say the least, not soundproof.

Our fellow tenants were treated to relentless loud hammering, drilling and sawing. Of course, Saul didn't hear a thing, not even the banging on the ceiling, or the pounding from the tenants underneath us, or on both sides of our apartment in protest to the deafening noise.

When the antique's interior was restored, all the neighbors of 670 Stone Avenue came to admire and toast to it, with our whole extended family. Schnapps and sponge cake were served.

Still the mystery remains; how did the antique end up in our kitchen, on Stone Avenue?

Sam, Esther, Sam

Esther Levine was made a widow by Uncle Sam, not America's Uncle Sam, but by Sam the mason.

He was the father of their 6 children. All were grown, themselves parents & grandparents. All had joined the mast exodus of white Brooklynites to the suburbs in the 1960's.

They left behind their aged immigrant parents in familiar Brooklyn, to "slightly" better neighborhoods. The area was adjacent to Brownsville but had less crime.

My Auntie Esther moved to East Flatbush into a ground floor apartment in a brick 3-family house. With her went her Victorian-styled brocaded sofa, two heavy carved armchairs of old-fashion horsehair, a mirrored credenza, and a pair of electrified cranberry glasses. What a rosy glow they emitted, falling on her collection of glass swans. A mahogany drum table held a lamp of two French lovers entwined in a forever embrace. I loved this dreamy room on Watkins Street so.

Now an elderly lady, she took her precious belongings and arranged them in her new place in East Flatbush. In her new apartment, she developed a pattern of leaving her window blinds up & open, except when she was undressed, or sleeping. Her lights were left on, too. This made her feel more comfortable in the strange flat.

Across the narrow driveway from her place was a twin building with an aged gent whom was a widower. He would try nonchalantly to watch Auntie Esther as she moved through her flat.

Their eyes would meet for a moment, then both would look away, quickly as if it didn't happen. This game went on for a month or two. Her male admirer was smitten. She was intrigued by the attention.

When this gent couldn't stand this hide & seek anymore, he asked Auntie Esther's landlady to introduce them. She was very shy having been married to my Uncle Sam since she was 15. Her silver-haired suitor had been married all his life. He too had his family all go out of Brooklyn. He was a brick-layer by trade.

It played out like a fairy tale. Once upon a time, Sam Watnick asked Esther Levine out with, "Maybe for a sandwich, Mrs. Levine, you could join me?" She coyly answered, "We'll see…

We'll see."

It took a while before she confided her secret love story to my mother, her sister. "You go, Esther, and NO you're not too old to fall in love!" Mom urged.

Maybe a few sandwiches later, an engagement ring appeared on Auntie Esther's finger. Then after some afternoon teas, they wed in her parlor.

They were surrounded by many children, grandchildren and other family members. He was the Prince, my new Uncle Sam… Auntie Esther the Princess. And they lived happily ever after, while holding hands in her enchanting parlor.

The Knish Konnection

I was alone in the bagel shop. It was 4:00 in the afternoon. This was after both the breakfast and lunch crowds. It was too early for the after-work crowd to grab a nosh, or for the arrival of the dinner patrons.

I had been shopping all day, and had not eaten lunch. When I passed my favorite Tal Bagel Shoppe I heard my stomach growl. In I went for a crusty, handrolled circle of bliss, topped with cream cheese.

I was savoring my last sip of coffee when another customer wandered in. The man was large in height and weight. He was about 250 pounds, African-American, in sweats and carrying bags of groceries. His eyes scanned the bountiful array of delicacies in the glass showcase. His mouth was visibly watering in anticipation of enjoying a special treat. Plopping wearily in a chair facing the counter, the man placed his bags on the floor. Then he placed a to-go order.

"Hey man, can I get one, no, better make it two, potato knishes? Slice them and give 'em plenty of mustard, okay?" he directed the Pakistani counterman, who then repeats the order, to make certain he heard correctly.

"Mustard on the knishes?" he asked incredulously, which I could see was odd request. The customer nodded, smiling.
"Could you put some extra mustard in the bag too? I just looove mustard on my knishes."
He then rose with an effort from his chair, took his groceries, paid for his order, and passed by my table as he tried to leave the restaurant. I couldn't restrain myself!

"You're from Brooklyn!" I accused the startled man. "Yeah, I am, how did you know that?" he replied, looking me over, squinting to see if he knew me. He didn't. We were perfect strangers.

"Anyone who would order a potato knish, cut open and smeared with mustard, is from old Brooklyn," I said. We both laughed. It turned out, after a few questions, he lived in the same Brownsville neighborhood I was from, but after I had moved away.

"That's when the Jewish people still lived there, that I learned to love knishes... with mustard," he said, nostalgically. "Remember all the kosher delicatessens in those days?" Every few blocks, there was one on the corner.

We screamed in unison that our favorite was Kisha King on Pitkin Avenue. As we reminisced, we became buddies. Me, a Jewish grandmother, he, in his 50's like my children. Joe Brown and I introduced ourselves and shook hands warmly. He told me how his grandfather, Marcus, came up north from Alabama in the 1940's. He settled in Brownsville to raise his family.

Joe knew the elementary school and the high school my siblings attended. We spoke of the Brownsville Recreation Center. I had been a member when it opened in the 1950's, and was called the Brownsville Boys Club. It was founded by Abe Stark, who never forgot growing up in our neighborhood. He became the borough president of Brooklyn.

Talk about coincidence, Joe Brown was presently a coach of the center's basketball team. He was trying to keep the kids out of trouble… Off the mean streets of today's Brownsville.

"Remember Betsy Head Pool?" he asked, breathlessly. "I'm on the mayor's committee to have it restored."
"Do I remember," I gushed. "My sister and I would pay 10 cents each, then receive an elastic bracelet with a locker key. We would swim the entire summer weather permitting."

In a brief few minutes, we covered the joy of our Brownsville, now but a memory for us, because it is probably the most crime-ridden neighborhood in New York. I mentioned that I had lived on Chester Street. "You lived on Chester, I lived on Bristol Street. It's on the next block!" he exclaimed. We were taken aback.

Joe and I shook hands, again, then bid farewell.
"Bye, see you!" He waved disappearing down into the subway.
"Enjoy your knishes with mustard," I shouted out to him. Brownsville was once a good place to grow-up…

A Hero's Cake

I love sweets—I guess that's why I always remember that white iced cake, topped with blue and red stars. My mother was NOT a good baker! See "Stone Cookies from Stone Avenue" for proof.

Still, she took upon herself to bake a splendored confection for my cousin, Irving Feinstein, a returning veteran of World War Two.

She stretched her limited skills, to religiously follow a Ladies' Home Journal recipe for this special occasion. It took Rose Diamond the better part of a day, but all her joy and patriotism were baked into the cake's layers. When it was delicately finished, our whole family marveled at its beauty… We salivated. To ensure it stayed pristine, she stashed it atop her highboy chest of drawers. This was meant to be a surprise we would share, after we picked up her nephew and his bride Jean from the airport.

I saw the orange lamplights of the Belt Parkway against the navy sky when my father drove us to Idlewild Airport in his 1937 Buick. I was lying down on someone's lap, half asleep, since it was past my bedtime.

"You were born, Dee-Dee dear, while our brave cousin was overseas, fighting to protect us," My mother said to me… Like I understood what overseas or war meant. Did it mean you got a delicious cake if you fought with your older sister, or brother, in a place called overseas?

There was much excitement and kisses (which I didn't care for), when the cousins landed, and I was shaken awake.

"Dee-Dee, wake up! Wake up, see who's here," the car full of relatives shouted.

All I could think of was Mama's red, white and blue cake waiting at home for us to eat...

Asparagus

Tonight, I made steamed asparagus and spaghetti for my lonesome dinner. Without warning, the sight of my plate triggered remanences of a childhood friend, Gloria Crespi. It was like a dream sequence, revisited.

The first time I ever ate asparagus was in her family's tenement apartment on Powell Street, in Brownsville. Mrs. Crespi served us spaghetti topped with Del Monte tomato sauce and asparagus on the same plate.

The avocado-green cut stalks from a can were exotic vegetables to me, and with spaghetti no less! How unique a dinner that was… So unlike my mother's usual heavy, greasy fare. It so impressed… I still remember that meal, in the old-fashioned, windowless kitchen.

Gloria, their only child, was always mischievous, adventurous and funny. She was not an ordinary, boring Brownsville girl, like the rest… Which why I enjoyed her. I guess she and I were not part of "clique," nor did we care to be. We were free to roam about Brooklyn afterschool, unconcerned and unwatched. Those were the safer, more innocent days of the fifties.

Gloria Crespi was a colorful figure of my elementary school days in the early 1950's. She was my best friend. On one trek behind the now-defunct Holland Steel Plant, she confided in me that she was adopted. Her parents adamantly denied it, even when she confronted them after spotting a document hidden in their bureau. Then it disappeared from the drawer. They insisted the certificate was a phony and that she didn't understand what she read… They insisted that she was their birth child.

When I relayed her secret to my parents, my mother declared, "Impossible… She looks just like her mother."

One summer Saturday, Gloria came to get me. She gleefully said, "My mother gave me a $5 bill, let's go to Coney Island and spend it!" You can't image what five whole dollars was worth in those days. "Lucky girl… you!" I shouted, as I hugged her.

It was one of the most exciting days of my life! We were about 10 years old then. Off we went onto the long subway ride to Coney Island, the Mecca of fun for Brooklyn youth. The subway ride was a nickel each.

The old IRT didn't go straight there, we had to transfer trains to the BMT line. The trip took about an hour & a half. We laughed and sang the whole trip in anticipation of the excitement ahead of us.

When we first arrived, we were starving, so we hit Nathan's for a hot dog, French fries and drink. I recall the franks were about 10 cents apiece. Now we were ready for all the rides and games of the Coney Island midway.

First the Cyclone rollercoaster, then the electric bumper cars, where we forcefully banged into the others, screaming in delight. This was followed by pink clouds of cotton candy.

The Fun House's distorting mirrors and shaking floors made us laugh, before the Ferris wheel beckoned. Gloria and I did whatever our young hearts desired, until we just had 10 cents left for the subway ride home, after ice-cream. By that time, we were nauseous and tired.

Next day, a distraught Mrs. Crespi called my mother to sob, "I don't know what to do with Gloria. She stole $5 from my purse... I'm at my wits end. Did you know that they went to Coney Island all by themselves to spend it all?" We got punished, but it was worth it! We remained pals thru the end of elementary school.

About two years after the Coney Island escapade, Gloria came over my house to tell me she got her period. In disbelief I followed her into our bathroom, where she showed me her soiled Kotex that was anchored with a sanitary belt. A few weeks later, surprise... I got my own first period too. We were 12 years old then.

Gloria and I graduated from elementary that June, in 1951. Her part of Brownsville went to one junior high, and mine to another. Now we hardly saw one another, we had new schools, new friendships.

Then I heard that her father died of a heart attack. Mrs. Crespi had to go to work. That's when Gloria was sent back to the orphanage, where she had gotten her as a baby.

I went to visit her in the "Home". She held on to me, while tears ran down her cheeks. "See, I told you I was not really their kid!" I cried each time I visited her, until my family moved out of Brooklyn.

Until this day, some 60 years later, I can't eat asparagus (especially with spaghetti), without wondering what happened to my friend Gloria Crespi.

The Warring Cans

They were neighbor landlords without much territory. To my father, his property's appearance meant pride of ownership. He was a normally quiet man who fought vigorously to protect its dignity.

In Brownsville, Brooklyn in the 1950's, my father and Mrs. Cohen each owned attached 3-story tenements on Loverdale Avenue, near the corner of Chester Street. Even their respective front doors almost touched, but for a narrow solid divide between the structures. They stood like maroon-shingled Siamese twins. On street level of each building was a store. The whole block was all joined tenements with different small businesses on the bottom.

My father's domain was one off the corner, and Mrs. Cohen's was the corner one. Sam Diamond had his kosher butcher shop with the Hebrew letters boldly painted on the windows. The numbers 292, and 294 in gold, were stenciled above the entrance to these 2 houses. Mrs. Cohen's store was rented as McCreed's Candy Shop.

The trouble started when my family bought #292 from the absentee former landlord. We moved into the first-floor apartment, and we had a tenant above us. Now my dad was in his store all day, and we lived above the shop.

We kept our metal garbage can covered on the far side of our doorway nearer the butcher shop. Mrs. Cohen insisted on placing hers on the side nearest our doorway. In order to enter our home we had to pass thru the pair of "receptacles of odorous delight". They straddled and guarded our castle.

When my father politely asked her to keep her refuse away from our side of the doorway, she answered rudely, "I was doing it this way for years, and I'll do as I damn please!"

Those were fighting words! So began the war of the garbage cans. Mrs. Cohen would park her garbage can on the other side of our doorway, and during the night my father would nosily drag it along the cement to where he felt it belonged. She'd come out of her house, cursing like the crazy woman she was, and move it back to where it pleased her. When she'd leave, my dad would haul it back again.

This went on for years, sometimes this activity would be practiced half dozen or more times a day. This was not hand-to-hand guerilla warfare, it was can-to-can garbage warfare!

Diamond and Cohen never called a truce... Eventually, my father retired and we moved away.

Brooklyn, Oh Brooklyn, Oh Brooklyn

This morning, I opened an unrequested, unwanted, unneeded catalogue of ladies' wigs, sent to my mailbox.

Can it be true? If only we had known and appreciated our dear ole Brooklyn more. What prompted this new coming of terms with the place that formed me, for better or worse?

Wh-hat, when did shabby-but-never-chic Brooklyn becomes the epitome of elegance, why did they chose to bestow a coiffured artificial head of hair with the name… "Brooklyn".

The Brooklyn moniker for babies, beer, pizza, etc. tickles me. "I Love Brooklyn" T-shirts abound on innocents, and punks alike attest to its glory. A hoity-toity Brooklyn Heights, Park Slope and Williamsburg neighborhoods for the successful, is not the Brooklyn I remember.

If you had a Brooklyn accent, that meant you were of an inferior breed, a creature of uneducated, immigrant parents. In my day, it was something you had to lose if you wished to ascend classes, to move up in the world.

I remember learning not to say "you's", instead you people, that "ain't" is not a word was drilled into our heads, to pronounce it "ask" instead of "ass-ed", library not "lie-berry", jewl-ry not "jew-el-ree". The accent was strong and defined, I guess like cockney in the UK, until the Beatles made it hip.

We were a family of first-generation Americans. We

lived in Brownsville, which is in south Brooklyn, and we were "poorish".

About once a month we would visit our poorer cousins, who lived in Williamsburg in a brownstone. I distinctly recall walking up the high brown, chipped cement steps to the double front doors. The interior stairway had gradually spiraled, worn steps, up to our cousin's third-floor rented apartment. Today, that once-shabby block of brownstones is worth millions, each.

I can't forget when my eccentric gay brother, Teddy bought a clapboard house in Park Slope some 30 years ago. The mixed-up interior had about five now-bare fireplaces, encased in pitted peeling plaster. The staircase to the second and third floor hung like loose trapeze ladders. One had to be out of their bloody mind to ever attempt climbing those swinging steps. Teddy, on the other hand, thought of himself as landed gentry. Before even doing important structural rehabilitation of the run-down staircase, he used his funds to have a stained-glass window of the family crest commissioned from one of his talented, but insane pals. It was installed on the second floor landing. This was so that when the sun's rays lit the colored glass, all who dared enter his shanty (I mean house), would know Lord Theodore resided there. From what shtetl this crest emerged, I can't imagine…

The family made fun of his decision, thinking he was crazy. The neighborhood was run-down, with derelicts and crime and filth. He told us that he wired pans and pots and bells across the attic, so that they would clang loudly if the druggies tried to climb in. I'm sure his method worked, and gave some would-be invaders the fright of their lives. I gather this was Teddy's version of an alarm system. This house was right next door to his artsy-fartsy friend, Randi, and he bought it for $19,000, since it laid idle for years. Thrown-out money, or so we his judgmental siblings thought.

Who's laughing today, after he sold it for more than a million, even after it was half-burnt down. This was caused by an old air conditioner he got from someone for nothing.

I recall when Teddy found a gas pipe in one of the hearths. He opened the ancient sealed valve with a wrench, and then lit the gas. The robust roaring flame in the brick kitchen hearth heated the whole place, one extremely fierce winter. When he received an enormous, appropriate gas bill from the utility company, he professed innocence. "How could I possibly make such a bill?" he asked them.

The visiting utility men were perplexed! They never could imagine how he could manage (as he claimed vehemently), to burn so much gas. How could anyone in their right mind think to do such a dangerous, wasteful and careless act? Over and over the crumbling clapboard house was checked for leaks and meter problems… To no avail! The utility company never found the cause, and wrote it off as a mystery. Teddy never had to pay that gas bill!

Writing of this event, I must relate the time Teddy called to tell me what a hard time he was going through emotionally. "My shrink wants to have a session, with

just you, concerning me and my problem. Will you go?"
How could I say no?
"Of course," I replied.

I made an appointment with his shrink. It is in a rough, high-crime area in a section of Brooklyn I do not know. Truth is, I feared for my life just entering that crime-stricken zone.

I drop my young daughters at their elementary school in a posh part of Long Island, and drive to the appointment. In those days of prosperity, I was driving a brand-spanking new Mercedes. I arrive after an hour's drive, and circle the doctor's block looking for a parking spot. About 15 minutes later I found a space. I then had a 45-minute session with the shrink, costing me $175.

The traffic I hit returning to Long Island had me in a panic. I was afraid I'd be late for my children's school dismissal. Luckily, I got there just in time.

Now Teddy phones me a few days later, and I tell him that I had the session with his shrink. Instead of hearing "thank you" from Teddy, he retorts,
"Oh, that schmuck... I don't go to him anymore!" This is a typical example of my annoying little brother, Teddy.

My father's three-story building, with a store on street level, was sold for $4,500.00 in the 1960's. Today the entire block of Riverdale Avenue is new two-family homes. His building and all the neighbors' were demolished to make way for these homes, after most were abandoned because of unpaid taxes by their landlords. This occurred after our area was flooded with unruly strangers, and crime soared.

There was a time, in 1965, when my husband, our baby girls and I moved to the South for business. I caught the flu, which landed me in the local hospital with pneumonia. My semi-private roommate was an aged Carolina mountain woman, who could not understand my accent at all. We both spoke English, but Brooklynese she had no experience with. We could not talk to each other at all!

During our residence in Charlotte, I took an art class at the community college. The teacher gave us an assignment to paint a picture of the tree in our front yard. I raised my hand and told all who would listen, "In Brooklyn where I grew up, there was only one tree on the entire block and that was in Mr. Margolis' yard. We were not allowed on his private property.

"Where's Brooklyn, anyway?" they smirked in their sugary, southern drawl. Ask the smirkers if they know Brooklyn now… SMARTASSES!

I would not be surprised if their offspring had a kid named Brooklyn… Or that they wished they lived there, or were transplants already. What a laugh!

My dream, and my Brooklyn contemporaries', was to grow up and move to Manhattan, which we Brooklynites referred to as the City. That was the Mecca of everything our Brooklyn was not… Fashionable, cultured, cosmopolitan… and affluent.

We did gleefully enjoy Coney Island, Prospect Park and the Zoo, the Brooklyn Museum, the Grand Army Library, Canarsie Pier, and Sheepshead Bay, where we went some summer nights, for fresh air and fishing. Also, Plum Beach, where we "watched the submarines," (a.k.a. parked and necked) as teenagers.

In 1955 when the "Bums" won the World Series, we excitedly ran to watch the spontaneous parade on Stone Avenue with packed convertibles, cars, bikes, wooden handmade scooters, with kids shouting, "We WON—We WON!" Horns and radios blasting... Such a celebration!

However, our Brooklyn hearts were totally broken, when our Brooklyn "Bums" (the Dodgers), were stolen from us. Beloved Ebbitt's Field, where they played ball, was insensitively sold to builders to be razed, and then covered in bland, towering buildings.

All of Brooklyn went into mourning! Truth is, this was the bell that tolled for our glory days in the borough (of course, in retrospect).

Saturday afternoons were spent in the magnificent palace-like movie theaters, with intricately-shelled serpent goldfish pools, in veined marble lobbies. The gold painted gargoyles and Juliet balconies, transported our imaginations to far off times and places. Its ceilings were stories tall, covered in navy velvet with miniature twinkling star lights. In the burgundy horsehair seats in the high balcony, I'd think I was in the heavens. I'd float out of this faux-baroque dream, my young head full of music and movie stars, to drab, tired Brownsville streets, with its worn tenements, and small immigrant-owned shops. I'd pass Brooklynites with so many different dialects as I walked the safe streets home.

It still hurts that the palaces of grandeur, our movie theaters, weren't landmarked. Imagine seeing, "Singing in the Rain", "One Touch of Venus", "Seven Brides for Seven Brothers", 'The Wild One", etc. in such fantasy surroundings. Is it a wonder that so many creative people emerged from our old Brooklyn, and all mention our theaters?

The nostalgic, crowded Belmont Avenue had its brother market street, Blake Avenue, of blocks of push carts of fruit and vegetables. Barkers touting their wares, and the fish markets with huge tanks of live, swimming fish to sell. Bras, girdles, bloomers, union suits and seamed hose as well as pots and pans were in the shops and stalls. Samples of their wares hung conspicuously.

My favorite was a very sour, garlicy pickle or crisp, green tomato wrapped in waxed paper, pulled from huge wooden barrels. It was perfect to munch on, while Momma shopped. Bakeries full of huge marble cheesecakes, sponge and honey cakes, pies and luscious rows of cookies. Braided challah, rye and pumpernickel and bagels and rolls of various shapes. The smells made our mouths water!

Diary stores where butter was carved from large vats, and cheeses aplenty sliced or scooped by hand. Burlap sacks of a variety of dried beans and nuts. Then there was the live poultry market to choose, then have ritually slaughtered and cleaned to order, chickens, duck and geese. The street color, the crowded untamed noisy mob of shoppers, babies crying in well-used carriages, peddlers peddling, women haggling for a bargain, made an entertaining theatre in ole Brooklyn.

Kosher and non-kosher butcher shops also lined its streets. Shoes, coats and every article of clothing were for sale. It was an agora/bazaar/mecca of shopping frenzy.

In the 1950's, the "government", a.k.a. Jacob Reis, decided to abolish this "slum". It was razed indiscriminately and completely, whole sections of streets and avenues, of our old but homey neighborhood. Its cracked sidewalks, which knew our footsteps walking, skipping or running, were gone. When I roller skated on its blocks, I knew just where every defect laid in my path. A game of avoiding obstacles made maneuvering more interesting than gliding on smooth boring concrete.

I remember the wrecked, torn down rubble of old bricks, chunks of concrete, painted walls, nails, smashed store front sections, rags that were once clothes, furniture limbs and broken everything that the wrecking balls produced. An all-out war was waged and won on the residents of my community. We became refugees moving to unfamiliar areas… Never, except in our memories, was there proof that *our* Brownsville ever was.

Nobody in Brownsville or adjacent neighborhoods knew where all the familiar displaced figures and family-owned businesses went. Our communities evaporated forever.

Now the projects that were built on our neighborhood soil loomed tall, boxy, the same offensive red uniform brick facades for blocks. Ugly, utilitarian monsters with strangers occupying them and changing our piece of Brooklyn. These mammoth projects cast dark shadows on the sunny days and forbidding dark spots at night.

Thank goodness, the wrecking ball missed our ivy-covered ancient brick public library. It's still there on a corner. I've seen it on Google.

I recall with deep affection the joy, comfort and knowledge it bestowed on me. The weekly "Story Hour" on the second floor, I never missed. I loved how the librarian, Miss Tremel, read us a story with such expression, and her lovely melodious voice. We knew she really loved her job.

Returning the books I borrowed on time and not losing my precious library card taught me responsibility. This is where I spent lonely afterschool afternoons, when my mother was working with my father, in his butcher shop on Blake Avenue.

Sometimes we hit the roller rink on Saturday to twirl in our plaid skating skirts and rented skates. What a let-down, leaving the movies to once more tread carefully past the looming, ugly projects that replaced the worn but endearing tenements and small businesses Brownsville was losing completely.

I'll bet the Gypsies who would suddenly appear living in vacant stores, don't visit yuppified Brooklyn, as they did when we were youngsters. Or the knish man pushing his coal fired tin oven/cart filled with goodies like potato or kasha knishes or crispy-skinned baked russet or sweet potatoes. Never to be seen again, the yellow candy apple cart. It was an enclosed glass box with two shelves, one held caramel dipped apples, the other red glistening apples.

Going downtown to Nevins Street, was agony and ecstasy for me as a youngster. I had to wait forever it seemed, while my mother shopped for the family, looking only for bargains. Only if we sat still and didn't whine constantly, I would be rewarded with a frosted sundae with hot fudge.

Most of the time I whined ruthlessly. I hated when she shopped for hours in the hot department stores, dangling the ever-not-worth-it treats.

Now it's not called downtown, but Park Slope, and it has a new famous sports center and a slew of huge office buildings. Gone are May's and A&S, Woolworth's, Lane & Bryant's and the bridal shop I bought my beautiful wedding gown in in 1959, for $80.

Gone was the famous Paramount Theatre where I saw all the great Rock n' Roll legends perform, while my peers and I danced furiously in its aisles. What fun we had!

After one show I saw Chuck Berry's white station wagon parked its lot, I wantonly took my 'Baby Pink"

lipstick and scribbled "I love you" all over it. Why…
because I was an out-of-control teenage fan. He came
running out of the Paramount screaming at me, "What
the hell you doin' girl?" The star was cursing mad…
Rightfully!

I was terrified and ran with my girlfriends down into
the subway station for our trip home. Memories,
memories. I'm 76 now but still I remember my run in
with Chuck Berry… And my precious youth spent in
dear ole Brooklyn.

60 Cents of Forbidden Exotic Pleasure

Secretly, we saved our meager allowances. When we had 60 cents we knew we could do the unthinkable! My sister and I went out for the afternoon, peacefully. She was five years my senior, 15, and I was 10.

Our mother should have known that we were up to something devious, because we left our tenement apartment without my sister rebelling loudly about me going anyplace with her. This was not the norm!

Today, we had a secret plan. We aimed in the direction of Sutter Avenue, over the neighborhood line dividing Brownsville from East New York. Surely no one would catch us there.

Sissy and I were the children of the neighborhood kosher butcher shop owner. We were always to be respectful Jewish children. Of course, we were only to eat kosher food, no dairy after meat for six hours, honor the Sabbath and all other Jewish holidays. It seemed it was always *erev* of some holiday, when we got a list of what we could and could not do on that occasion.

It was scary, sinful and rebellious, what mischief we were up to! Then we saw the garish red painted storefront with the Chinese writing on its foggy window. Sheepishly, we opened the double door, to the strange food smells of the Orient.

I looked around to make certain no one saw us enter this place that might cost us "Eternity in Hell". The bowing Chinese waiter quietly asked, "Yes, you's here for da lunch?"

"Y-yea," we now very American cool kids, or so we now thought, nodded. He sat us at a booth with a red plastic covered tablecloth. We stared at the odd selection of 60-cent lunch specials.

Soon the busy waiter returned to take our order. Sissy said, "We'll be sharing one combination lunch. Let us have the #3—Tomato egg-drop soup, egg roll, and fried rice with lobster sauce. Sissy added with authority, "Then for dessert we'll have kumquats!"

I was impressed with my elder sister's worldliness! "B-but how did you know what to order?" I asked.
"I didn't!" she admitted, while kicking me under the table. We ate every morsel with such relish and guilty pleasure. I wish I could enjoy such an experience today!

Papa

My mother and father didn't argue. The way we kids knew our parents had a disagreement of sorts, was the "Silence Plague".

Papa would take an offense to something my mother said, or did, and she would declare, "Papa's *shein tsebeyzen!*" That meant literally, "now Papa's blown-out angry". After some mysterious insult, or a disrespectful act, we the whole family would brace for what lied ahead... That meant he would not utter a single word to my mother until the unknown insult was rectified to his satisfaction, or he became *nokh tsebeyzen* of his own free will. In the meantime, we kids suffered from an irritating inconvenience.

It was hard to settle his grievance because my mother couldn't imagine what she did wrong. This is the exact opposite of airing one's problems. Selfishly we wished they slug it out and get over it!

My two siblings and I would be caught in the middle. We'd be called on relaying each of their one-sided conversations back from one, to the other. It drove us batty! The back and forth would operate something like this:

Papa: "Tell your mother the mail was picked up."
Mom: "Tell your father, I know because I picked it up."

Papa: "Tell your Mama I'm ready for supper."
Mom: "Inform your Papa to SIT AT THE TABLE ALREADY."

Papa: "Remind your Mama its *Erev Yontif*, and to let your Papa know what to bring from the store for her to prepare for the table."

Mom: "Clearly let him know I'll need an end of steak, and a pullet and some soup bones."

Papa: "How many pounds does she need?"

Mom (losing patience): "Tell your father to use his head, we'll be 7. He should remember he invited his landsmen (friends from the old country), Shmuley and Abraham, too."

Papa: "Ask your Mama where she put my winter union suit, the old soft one, not the itchy new one she bought me that I don't need."

Mom: "Advise your father, Mr. Diamond where I always put them… In the bottom drawer of the bureau."

Papa: "And while Mrs. Diamond is looking… Let her find my favorite scarf that your Auntie Rachela knitted for me."

This frustrating nonsense could go on and on. The fact most frustrating for us human walkies-talkies was that they each plainly heard one another's words, since we all inhabited the same cramped tenement apartment.

Papa's *tsebeyzen* is pocketed throughought my childhood memories of family life with Papa and Mama, in Brownsville.

A Lesson from Mom

Terrified, I scampered under my parent's bed. I was about seven years old. I wasn't sure how I had so angered my mother that she ran for the tin can of black pepper to teach me a lesson I'd never forget.

I had innocently repeated a word I heard some tough kid shouting in the playground, to ask her what it meant. This infuriated her like I had never remembered in my short life.

Usually when she hollered at me for something I did wrong, I would run under the bed until she got over it. Then timidly I'd sneak out when I thought she forgot about what I did. This time, I had really crossed the line because she stripped the double bed, mattress and all, and ran for the wooden broom. My mother poked the wooden handle between the metal springs (all beds had metal springs in the 1940's), until I was forced out from under the shelter of the bed and into her grasp. She held me down forcefully and poured the black pepper into my howling mouth, and it accidently got into my little brown tearing eyes.

I am 74 years old now, but still hesitate fearfully to say the word that caused me and my mother such distress… "FUCK."

Today I watch TV, go to the movies, walk in the supermarket and hear "FUCK," and "FUCKIN' this or that," and even "motherfucker" peppered throughout. All ages use the word freely it seems. Momma must be spinning in her grave!

The Diamonds Hit Charlotte

First impressions were so important to him. Success breeds success. This was my husband's mantra.

That's why we moved into the white pillared brick duplex on Dresden Drive, when we were relocated to Charlotte. That's also why Howard's showy white Cadillac graced the circular driveway before the front door. We joined the "right" country club and wealthy Reform temple. Our toddler attended the "elitist" nursery school. Our little daughters and I wore easily recognizable, monogramed whenever possible, expensive clothes. Of course, Howard donned the beautiful menswear that he represented in the territory.

I had to admit we cut quite the prosperous, attractive family anyone would be honored to know. Until…

My parents, the Diamonds of Brownsville, Brooklyn, decided to visit their splendid family, us. This was during their motor trip to Miami Beach for the winter.

My dear old folks pulled into our highly visible driveway, right smack dab up to our ornate red lacquered door, with the antique lion's head brass knocker.

Since they arrived on a Friday morning, way before The Sabbath that evening, my husband Howard was still away on his weekly road sales trip. He was due home early that evening.

How do I describe my feelings, that day?

1. I was overjoyed to see my Mommy and Daddy… I missed them so in this unfamiliar southern city. I was lonely.

2. My babies were thrilled to see their Bubbie and Zeyde, and relished their spoiling attention.

But my stomach sunk when I viewed what my husband's eyes would behold. "Oy," I said to myself, as I mentally smacked myself in the head. Their old Buick was hand-painted black. A spare tire was tied with a rope on its round hump top. The auto was used as their covered wagon to transport them, and all comforts, to Florida. Thus, it was filled with quilts, pillows, clothing and greasy brown bags of home-prepared food.

My neighbors Jenna and Jimmy Flowers were given gifts of giant kosher salamis, which they had never seen before, straight from Brooklyn, which they didn't know existed. For this act of kindness, Jenna immediately cooked up a huge batch of fried okra which we had never seen or eaten before.

Jimmy said in his distinctive son-of-a-tobacco-farmer drawl, "I can eat it on white bread, with lotsa butter, lettuce, tomato and sweet pickles… And only if I don't allow myself to think about what's it's made of." We felt about the same of Jenna's crispy, yet slimy okra!

I wish I had a picture of Howard's face when he pulled into our prestigious neighborhood, and spotted this scene straight out of the Beverly Hillbillies.

Two Knees

"Sam I can't stand it! Stop it right away!" she begged. But to no avail.

"Rosie let me be! Can you?" he answered, adjusting his slipping yarmulke due to the commotion on his lap.

It was a scene of loving bedlam, when my hovering mother fed her visiting grandchildren and their grandfather. This was after a full day at Miami Beach. The girls had cajoled their Zeyde to carry one of them in each arm, while they splashed and frolicked in the ocean. At the same time, he would amuse them with stories of me and my siblings, from when we were little like them. "More... More, tell us more!" they pleaded, not letting him catch a breath.

On the walk back from the shore they eyed a neighborhood candy store, and made him promise candy after supper. But to stop their whining he would promise them anything... And they knew it.

My waiting mother, the Bubbe, gave them showers and steered them, all cleaned up, to the dinner table. One little granddaughter was planted on each of my father's 73 year old knees.

They were seated at the flowered, oilcloth-covered table in the teeny dinette, with only a wee breeze slipping thru the old screen door. This small space in my parents' vacation home had an aura and smell of Jewish Russia/Brownsville/Miami uniqueness, all its own. Its irregular walls were plastered with photos of these children, prominent amongst outdated family pictures from yesteryear. There were faded black and white pictures of children since grown up, amongst those long-gone in this collage of frozen moments.

The aroma was of food that took hours to simmer on the minute stove tucked in the kitchenette. In its half window above the one-legged tub sink, hung wind chimes and cutesy fruit-motif curtains. A pair of smiling, male and female plastic chef faces adorned its only piece of wall. This was in my parents' ground floor apartment on Euclid Avenue, in old Miami Beach circa the early 1960's.

Both my youngsters were squeezing the food placed on Zeyde's plate thru their little fists, then eating some, and feeding him too. Need I describe what a mess this all made? My father, their Zeyde, was quelling with utter joy, the little ones giggling food particles all over their chubby, sun-kissed cheeks. It also landed in their mops of curly blonde hair.

Their grandma was frustrated that the meal she slaved over all day was being treated like Play-Doh. Such disrespect! She also knew they'd need bathing again, her chore, no doubt. The apartment would require her elbow grease to get it back to her spic-n'-span liking after this meal. What a job!

"Rosie, dear, please understand my food tastes sweeter sharing it with them this way," was my father's only explanation. My girls took it all in, smirking. This upset my mother, when she was cast as the "mean" grandparent, while he was the adoring, fun one.

Following this meal, after baths, and in PJ's, the girls would drag him to the candy store (their shared secret), all the while wailing, "PLEASE, PLEASE! You promised, you promised us candy—We want candy!" They wouldn't stop until they got just what they wanted. They knew Bubbie wouldn't approve, but Zeyde indulged them anyway.

My father had the patience of a saint when it came to Elissa, named for his revered mother, and Dawn, for his brother Henry. Zeyde made everything fun and games for his little girls. The day began early, at 6:30, for them and their grandfather. Bubbie would sleep late.

Breakfast started their food games, for which I would pay the price, once we got back home to New York.

Oranges and grapefruits were cut-up and called soldiers, to get them to eat them as the "War of the Fruits" was played on their shared plate. The losing "soldiers" got eaten, one by one.

Fried eggs were scrambled in butter and then became golden crumbs. They cleaned the plate of eggs willingly. Any bread crusts left on their dishes were fed to the birdies that waited on the fence out their creaky screen door. The little ones loved the colorful group of birdies that gathered, and they seemed to know Zeyde. To say my father over-indulged my daughters is an understatement. They adored him and he them, that is until…

On the last day of the grandkids' visit, the youngest pushed even her Zeyde to his limit! The girls had knocked out their old grandfather after a very humid, exhausting afternoon at the beach, with the presently very spoiled, out-of-hand little imps. The three of them shared his lunch plate, but while the girls were wildly jumping on and off his aching lap. Then he made the mistake of taking an unplanned siesta, in his chair on the porch.

The two girls were playing beauty parlor quietly, when they looked at my father's long wad of steel-colored hair, which he would carefully comb over his bald head. Elissa and Dawn went to work. Whose idea it was, we'll never know.

Sometime later, they gleefully woke Zeyde, by sticking his wife's mirror in his face. "Look Zeyde, look how pretty we made you!"

It took a moment for him to realize they had gotten scissors and cut off his precious combover tress… to its roots. Now even my over-indulgent, patient father had had enough! It would take him a good year to regrow that crop of precious hair. He went bonkers!

My mother on the other hand…. She laughed so hard, she cried!

The Working Stiff's Paradise of Yesteryear

It vanished like a dinosaur, hit by a comet. It can never come back... But it's a part of New York history. Those of us lucky enough to have enjoyed its uniqueness, the joy it brought, the memories of fresh air, sea, sand and sharing of families' intimacies, has never been duplicated.

It afforded us a sheltered community free of smut, smokestacks and pollution, relief from the crowded, hot city streets. As I remember it, no one was ever lonely in this neighborly setting.

"Chateau Warsaw" was in the Rockaways, near others like it. It stood one block from Rockaway Beach.

A weathered, wood-shingled three-story structure, with a wrap-around porch and high stoop. The trim and multi-paned windows were stark white. A dozen ancient rocking chairs sat invitingly. The front garden was filled with mature lilac bushes. Their powerful perfume drifted up (at the slightest breeze) to the generous porch.

A hand-painted sign swung over the entrance: Rooms for Rent—With Cooking Privileges.

Oscar Baer, a German immigrant, built the house with his own skilled hands. That was about 1925. Both him and his American Dream, "Heidelberg House," would prosper forever... So he thought. But Oscar got old. He got tired of catering to lodgers and the upkeep. So, he sold his "baby" to a Polish immigrant, Eli Kaplan in 1950, and retired to Florida.

This place, now re-named, remained an affordable summer respite for the immigrant classes of Brooklyn, the Bronx and Lower East Side. Since it was a subway ride from home, they flocked our way, to secure a piece of summer delight.

Our "Chateau Warsaw" boasted 13 bedrooms and three bathrooms, one to each floor. Every one of the 13 rooms had a different family occupying it. Some of the larger rooms had as many as three beds and even a crib squeezed in. A small room might be for a couple or a single elderly person.

Each floor having only one bathroom was challenging, believe me! Many times, during the night you could hear people scampering to another level, if a necessary bodily function couldn't wait for relief.

On street level, the high basement held our community kitchen for all boarders to use. Its walls were white-washed cement, lined with basement windows on two sides. These were dressed in red polka-dot curtains.

The freshly painted red cement floor was a cheerful stage for this bustling, noisy food arena. This community kitchen was cleverly appointed. There were 13 numbered, individual stall-like closets, with a refrigerator and shelves, for groceries and pots, dishes, etc. They were lined up, on the opposite solid walls

Set against one of the windowed walls, were 13 burners on a gas stovetop and three deep utility-size sinks. These were ample for our boarders to prepare their meals.

Running down the middle of this community space, were 13 red and white checkered oilcloth-covered tables, with chairs. On each family table, a paper napkin holder and a five-and-dime glass vase, with a white plastic rose.

A festive flair was further lent to our community kitchen/dining-room by an ancient, slightly-out-of-tune, upright piano often played by Miss Axelrod, a retired schoolteacher. She might be accompanied by Eli Kaplan, Host and Warsaw-trained violinist. I have warm memories of that cavernous, yet homey room.

It seems to me, those past summer days were always sun-filled. Families armed with blankets, bagged lunches, toys and youngsters in tow beat a path to the nearby beach. The sea was always rough in the Rockaways, but so much fun. The children held onto the ropes, jumped and squealed in delight with each wave. Usually, we didn't return to the Warsaw Chateau until early evening.

Sandy and still wet, we would wait our turn to wash-off, in the wooden, enclosed shower in the backyard. No sand dared enter our establishment, see the posted rules!

Then it was time to sit down to supper at your own table, and hungrily devour your mother's cooking. Of course, we would check out what others were eating. A lot of cross-tasting went on, recipes were compared and adopted.

After dinner clean-up, we were beckoned to the wooden boardwalk. It was miles long in those days and only a block away from our residence.

The Atlantic Ocean was foamy as it crashed loudly, against the huge rocks of the jetties. Endless spans of sand and a dark sea, with the moon's reflection casting a path to the horizon. It was both magical and medicinal at the same time.

Can you imagine, what this sight meant for the tenement-dwellers myopic eyes, or the fresh, clean sea breezes that filled their lungs?

We'd stroll easily to 35th Street, because it had an arcade of games, carnival rides and food concessions. It was always crowded and noisy in a most festive way.

One always had room for frozen custard, a hot dog, French fries, a slice of pizza, a soft salty pretzel or–the piece de resistance—one (or more) mouth-watering Jerry's knishes. What a choice... potato, kasha, cherry or blueberry cheese?

Writing about Jerry's Knishes, I chuckle remembering being pregnant with my first child and yearning all day only for them. I couldn't eat a thing all that day. Impatiently, I waited for when my husband would return from work and walk with me to Jerry's.

Of course, we hit the place. I devoured about six knishes, one after the other, to his amused amazement! I paid for it with heartburn that lasted the rest of my pregnancy.

As a bride of 18 years old, that first summer we lived in the house, the older housewives would teach me how to cook

Friday mornings were the most frantic, as all were preparing for the best meal of the week. The aromas drifted thru the entire establishment and out to the porch. Our mouths watered in anticipation of the evening Sabbath meal.

Even husbands that were absent during the week came home for Sabbath, when we would be a full house, truly.

On Friday night, we lit Sabbath candles. That's when we all ate our special dinner. Chicken soup, cholent, pot roast, vegetables, and compote. Challah, cake or pies were bought in the 67th Street market, because our community kitchen had no ovens.

Since every family had its own food and was responsible for cooking it alone, thus this configuration became affectionately called a "Chook-Alane" by its immigrant Jewish guests.

Those sweet, bygone summers… in The Warsaw Chateau, on Beach 46th Street, will always be a smile in my heart.

So That's the Way the Pizza Slices

"Pizza, Pasta & Pastry" read the red/yellow/green neon sign, flashing like a traffic light, over a narrow Italian storefront circa 1960 in Flatbush. This Italian/Jewish neighborhood was in the beginning throes of an ethnic upheaval. So were the generations of the Italian-American family owners of this eatery. Love, betrayal, scandal, families and childhood friendships shattered and eight children, six parents and 12 grandchildren were baked in this Sicilian pie. It would be sliced and re-sliced.

John, Bruno, Thomas and Priscilla grew up together. They lived on Osborne Street, in Brooklyn, attended the same Catholic school, and were like an extended family. Holidays like Easter and Christmas were celebrated visiting door to door, between their small houses. The cookie cutter houses had the same vintage gnarled fig tree, in every napkin-sized front lawn. All had a tiny rear yard, where grapevines crawled over a lattice arch. In the summertime, this provided welcome cool shade to sit under, and delicious wine all year. All were first generation Americans, in a close-knit community, wrapped around Saint Vincent's Church and Sicilian regional old traditions.

Thomas

Thomas Russo met a vivacious Polish-American girl named Stella, at a Catholic dance club. The pair dated only a short time, as Stella lived all the way in the Bronx. The Bronx commute constituted a very long subway ride from Brooklyn. Thomas & Stella had a small wedding. They moved into a neighborhood apartment, above a liquor store in Flatbush. Thomas's grandfather owned this tenement building, on Bristol Street, only blocks from Osborne Street.

Nine months later, Stella gave birth to a baby girl. They baptized Dawn-Marie in St. Vincent's, surrounded by family and all us buddies.
Thomas Russo is a hard-working plumber assistant who puts in long hours. Stella would be at home with their baby, Dawn-Marie. She was young, pretty, and stayed the wild 19-year-old who so captivated him.

Eventually Stella started hanging out in the liquor store, on the street level of their apartment house. She was bored and lonely. Tony Rico, the shop's manager, was a handsome, smooth-talking ladies' man. An exciting contrast to her predictable, thus dull husband, Thomas.

One not so fine evening, Thomas comes home to find baby, Dawn-Marie in her crib, alone in the apartment. There's a note on the kitchen table from Stella.
Tom, I left with Tony… We're off to our new life, in California. He's married too, but we're so in love. Tony plans to divorce, I will also… And we'll be together. Then as an afterthought: *Dawn-Marie needs dinner. Ciao!*

A sobbing, broken Thomas called his "brother" Sunny to come quickly. He is lost, and alone with his upset baby. Sunny comforted his friend and brought the child home to his wife for the next few days.

They decided together, with his distraught father, to have Dawn-Marie and him to move into their house. Thomas gives up the flat he, Stella and their child shared. He works days, then takes over care of his child in the evenings. Devotion and love he showers on his wee daughter…she is his life.

Sunny Milano

At the Russo's wedding, Sunny had found his love. Me, Bella, a Jewish girl from the bordering Brownsville neighborhood. Sunny and I got married after we both got raises at our first jobs. We could then afford to pay rent for a walkup apartment, also in Flatbush. We childhood friends, were married couples… And as close as ever.

Priscilla

Priscilla Romeo was typically kept under her domineering mother's apron. She scrubbed and cooked for her large family of parents, single uncles and younger siblings.

No socializing with boys nor hanging out with girlfriends. School, church and family… Period. In Priscilla's senior year of high school, Bruno started to call on her, with their parents' approval. He grew up in the house next door. When Priscilla and Bruno finished school, they married as their families orchestrated. They were each other's only experience with the other sex. Just like back in the old country.

Priscilla's father Giuseppe was a chef all his life. It was his wedding gift to his daughter and son-in-law to setup this neighborhood restaurant, so they could earn a living. It was Giuseppe who even named the place.

Each night Giuseppe Romeo would make the dough ready for the next day, for the couple to fry and bake. After a time, a baby boy named Marco was born. Priscilla's mother Carmella babysat, while Priscilla worked with Bruno in their bustling business. It was a smooth, efficient family operation.

Now comes the tsunami that started almost simultaneously, that swept away the villains, along with the victims. Generations were thrown about. They landed disoriented, but realigned on other shores.

One not so fine day, Bruno lands in the hospital. We friends are not told about his stay or for what reason he was in there. But after his two-week-long stint, he does not return to Priscilla, their baby son nor to the Pizza, Pasta, & Pastry Shop.

Bruno checks out of his home, and checks in with the African-American nurse he met in the hospital. Forget the hurt of infidelity, this was also the early 1960's, when Italians did not intermarry. The families were deeply ashamed, devastated at how could Bruno do this.

All were punched, cut, baked and fried just like Giuseppe's dough! Bruno, the rebel, wasted no time. He filed for a divorce from Priscilla, abandoned Marco and completely severed family ties. All he wanted was his clothes from their apartment, and his nurse.

Now his son was emotionally and financially dependent on Priscilla, his single mother. She started running the business solo. Her heartbroken parents assumed total care of the baby, while she slaved away earning a living, keeping Pizza, Pasta & Pastry going. It had become a warm favorite in our neighborhood. The place was open from six in the morning to ten at night.

As the Pie Slices

Occasionally, Thomas stops off at his friend Priscilla's place, to see how she's doing. He'll bring some pastries and pizza home after work with him. The childhood pals cry their hearts out and learn to lean on one another for support. They can't understand how their lives turned. Bruno, Thomas and Priscilla were all Bristol Street kids.

Since their toddlers were about the same ages, occasionally they would take their kids out together. Sometimes they would go to a movie or just keep each other company, they were both so lonely. They kept this a secret between them.

One fine day they married quietly in city hall, with just children and grandparents present. The following Sunday, over a delicious supper in the Pizza, Pasta & Pastry Shop, they announce to us, their oldest, dearest friends, the marvelous news. We couldn't have dreamt a better outcome. Tears and kisses flowed, what a lovely rebirth for us all!

Priscilla and Thomas had a ready-made family with a boy, Marco, and a girl, Dawn-Marie. Priscilla sells her eatery to a new immigrant family. She is to be a full-time mother now, as Thomas insisted.

They moved to Staten Island into a single-family home. Then they are blest with an additional two children, Sophie and Carmine. The Russo Clan is a loving, happy, busy household.